THE
CONSEQUENCE
GIRL

I AM WOLF

ALASTAIR CHISHOLM

nosy
crow

First published in the UK in 2024 by Nosy Crow Ltd
Wheat Wharf, 27a Shad Thames,
London, SE1 2XZ, UK

Nosy Crow Eireann Ltd
44 Orchard Grove, Kenmare,
Co Kerry, V93 FY22, Ireland

ISBN: 978 1 83994 531 1

A CIP catalogue record for this book will be available from
the British Library.

Printed and bound in Great Britain by Clays Ltd, Elcograf S.p.A.
following rigorous ethical sourcing standards.
Typeset by Tiger Media

Papers used by Nosy Crow are made from wood grown in
sustainable forests.

1 3 5 7 9 10 8 6 4 2

www.nosycrow.com

For Sarah, who is a little bit Wolf
A.C.

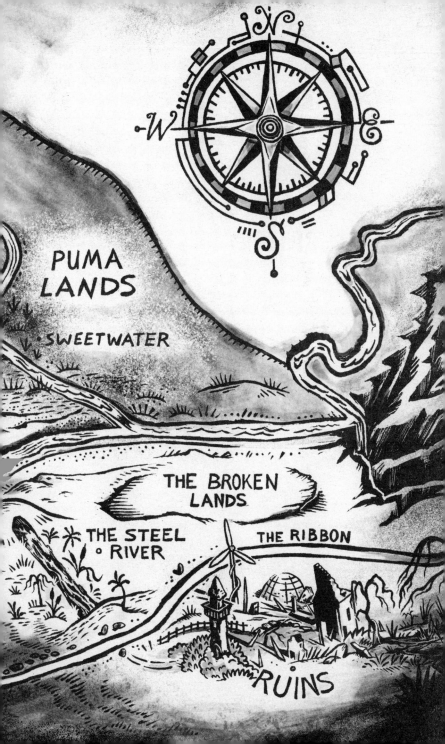

PROLOGUE

The great steel Wolf loped across the land, and death was in her eyes.

She was thirty metres high at the shoulder; each leg was as wide and tall as a tree trunk, and the barrel of her body was fifty metres end to end. Pistons and servos charged as she moved, metal sliding over metal, cables pulling, motors whirring, and upon her back her crew of humans cheered and roared. Her eyes glowed yellow and sharp, and her teeth shone silver.

Ahead of her, Hyena limped and struggled. Hyena was as large as Wolf, with a tough metal hide, and he was quicker than he seemed. They'd fought several times already, vicious snarling scraps that had left both damaged. Twice Wolf had closed her jaws round his neck, and twice he had reared, twisted, escaped. Once he had caught her between his own bone-crushing teeth and nearly ended her.

But Wolf was clever, and lightning fast. Her steel claws were sharp as razors, her eyesight keen, her shoulders powerful. And her faith was strong. She was Wolf! Ghost of the forest, scourge of the tundra, lone destroyer, Wolf! Her crew were many, her will indomitable! Wolf!

She had chased the enemy Construct for days, through woodland, over hills, across plains. She was patient and careful, never letting her prey rest, never letting him get too far ahead. Now, as the sun set on the third day, they were nearing the end, and her crew knew it.

"WOLF!" they roared. "WOLF!"

Hyena clambered to the top of the next hill, gasping. Wolf sensed his fear. Her vast mouth opened and she laughed.

"WOLF!" she heard. "WOOOOOOOOOLF!"

Wolf felt her crew. She felt them. Every little human gave her strength, their energy feeding into her, beating through her silver veins. *We are Wolf*, she felt. *We are Wolf*. Her hind legs fired like springs, and she leapt! Her claws raked Hyena's back, her teeth fastened round his neck, and her huge spring jaws clamped shut!

Hyena kicked at her as they tumbled into the next valley. His weight crushed her, but she didn't let go. She felt his armoured hide buckle. She could see his crew now, the tiny humans panicking and scrambling around, and, as their faith faltered, his strength drained away. He was growing weak, while she was still strong!

Then Hyena twisted and somehow loosened Wolf's grip, rolling until her jaws slipped from his neck to his shoulder. Wolf felt the crunch of steel and the spark of electrical systems exploding – but it wasn't the killing blow, and now she was off balance. She slipped, and the muddy ground collapsed beneath her, sending her reeling.

Furious, she scrambled back to her feet. Hyena was moving again. He was badly injured, limping worse than before; the sparks and fires on his shoulder lit up the night, and pieces of his casing lay scattered on the ground. Humans too – fallen from his deck, shaken loose from their harnesses, lying still or running for cover.

Wolf raced forward, feeling her crew's excitement. One more attack and he would be down, she knew. One more!

But Hyena was heading towards the end of a spit of land, and suddenly Wolf realised what he was trying to do. She snarled in fury and chased. She was only metres away from him! His right shoulder was ruined, he could barely move, his crew were weak, *he* was weak, he was prey!

"WOLF!" shouted her crew.

She leapt and her steel front paws stabbed at his hindquarters. She pressed down with all her weight and Hyena staggered once, twice, then his back legs collapsed – he was down!

And then he rolled, righted himself, tipped forward – and disappeared.

Wolf shook her head in fury, and then carefully stepped forward. Ahead, the ground vanished into a steep slope. Hyena was sliding and scrambling down, out of control. He rolled, then splashed into the river below. The sound of his fall echoed around the land, the water, the *boom* as he hit, the shriek of twisting metal and the shouts of his crew.

He lay in the river, motionless. For a moment, Wolf wondered if he was dead. But then he shook his head and got to his feet, and his lights glowed dimly in the dusk. He didn't try to climb out of the water. Instead, he stumbled forward and let the current carry him downstream.

Wolf growled. On board, her crew swore. Should she follow him? She wanted to. But the cliff was deadly, and the river too. And it marked the end of Wolf territory, and the start of Puma. She would not want to face both…

She shook her head and slowly regained her calm. Hyena was gone. Maybe Puma would get him. Maybe he'd escape. But he'd never dare come back to her lands again. She padded back the way she had come, feeling the triumph of her crew, hearing their laughter. The scattered metal and parts of Hyena's shoulder were still lying around as a prize, and the humans…

The humans would either join her crew or be left on the ground as Worms. The parts would be used for her own repairs. Wolf padded up to the top of the hill and smiled a wide-mouthed grin to the night sky, her long metal tongue lolling.

"Wolf," her crew called. "*Wolf. Wolf! WOOOOOLF!*"

Wolf laughed, threw back her head, and howled at the moon.

1

COLL

The ground was always *weird*.

Coll could never get used to how it didn't move under his feet. On board Wolf, the decks were always shifting, swaying as she paced, even as she slept, and Coll's body swayed with her by habit. But the ground was hard and unmoving. It made him feel like he was about to tip over. And it was too low down, so the world seemed to curve up as if he was standing at the bottom of a bowl. And it didn't smell right. And it was *dirty*.

He scraped mud off his boots and looked around. It was early morning; Wolf was half asleep, stretched out on the ground with her eyes closed and her huge steel ears twitching. Coll could feel her in his mind, the giant mechanical Construct. She was enjoying the sunshine and paid no attention to the humans crawling over her, cleaning her, mending her, smoothing out her woven

6

metal pelt. As she breathed, her sides moved, and the deck moved, and her humans moved. Coll, from the ground, watched them enviously.

"Hoy, dozy!" He turned, and a canvas sack hit him in the face. Luna grinned at him. "Get to work."

Coll grinned back and they headed tailside. The remains of last night's battle with Hyena covered the hill and now all the youngsters were on salvage duty. Luna skipped ahead and Coll followed her. She was the same age as him but shorter; since his twelfth birthday, Coll seemed to have stretched like a telescope and now he was a clear head taller than her. She was still faster.

They got to work. Most of the debris was Hyena's, ripped away by Wolf's massive jaws. Huge thick hairs made of burnished metal, electronics, hexagonal carbon-fibre panels – it could all be reused. Most valuable of all were the tiny scraps and dribbles of anthryl, dark silver, glinting in the sunlight. Anthryl was the incredible, magical material that held everything together, gave them life. Panels and cables could be replaced, but without anthryl there would be no Wolf. It moved in Coll's hands like grainy liquid metal.

They worked for an hour, searching and scavenging, until Luna stood and stretched. "That's two sacks – let's head back."

"There's something in that tree," said Coll, pointing. "Give me a minute." He wandered across and started to climb.

"Are you OK doing that?" asked Luna.

Coll grunted. "Course I am." He heaved himself up to the first couple of branches.

"Do you want a hand?"

He felt her lifting his foot and shook her off. "No, stop fussing."

"You know what Alpha said—"

"I can climb a *tree*," he snapped, and she stopped. He clambered through the branches and found some casing fragments, nothing special. He knocked them to the ground and leaned against the trunk, catching his breath. Despite his bravado, his left elbow was aching, and his knee too, though he wouldn't admit it. The tree swayed and swished in the morning breeze. It was a little like being on Wolf. Coll smiled. He turned to come down, and then he saw it, lodged between two branches.

A tooth.

It was one of Wolf's, ripped from her mouth during the fight. A metre long, sharp at the tip and shimmering with anthryl. Coll knocked it loose and it landed with a heavy *thud*. When he scrambled down, Luna was examining it with delight.

8

"A whole *tooth*!" she exclaimed. "Nice find!"

Coll grinned. "Come on, let's go."

They dumped the sacks with the rest of the salvage and carried the tooth headside, finding one of the Tocks working on Wolf's shoulder. The Tocks were the ones who kept Wolf running. That's what they liked to say, anyway, although Coll had never seen them foraging for equipment or food, or taking part in battles. This one was Intrick, a dour old man who never said much. When he saw the tooth he grunted and jerked a thumb up towards the mouth, where a lone figure was working, peering at a device in her hand. As Coll and Luna approached, the figure turned and stared at them.

"Something useful at last, then," she said.

"Good morning to you too, Rieka," said Luna.

The girl ignored her and scanned the tooth. Coll and Luna exchanged glances.

Rieka was the same age as them but always gave the impression of being an old and crotchety adult in a young person's body. Her skin was brown, darker than Coll's, and her short black hair stuck up on one side. Her face was a sharp triangle. Everyone said she was a genius – she'd only joined Wolf a year or so ago, but already even the adult Tocks listened to her. She had a reputation for getting annoyed with idiots. Coll suspected her definition

9

of 'idiots' was 'everyone'.

She reached up to Wolf's ear and murmured something. Wolf stretched her mouth open in a wide yawn, and her huge steel tongue lolled out on the grass. There was a gap where the tooth should be, dark and rough as if torn.

"Come on, then," snapped Rieka.

Coll heaved the incisor into the gap and held it steady as Rieka tapped her device. The base of the tooth moved. The dark silver anthryl coating shifted and remoulded itself to fit, moving like a snake, or water, or both. It wrapped itself round the base, and within a few seconds it was as if the tooth had never been gone.

Wolf's mouth suddenly twitched, and Coll leapt away before the jaws closed with a *snap!*

"Argh!" he gasped.

Rieka ignored him. Intrick came along, and the two Tocks looked at their devices and talked the fast complex Tock speak that no one else understood.

"You're welcome," called Luna.

Neither looked up. Luna and Coll exchanged another look, and then shrugged and left. Coll rubbed his elbow.

"She nearly got you that time," said Luna, clapping her hands together. "*Chomp!*" She reached for a cable hanging down from Wolf's deck and tugged it twice, and it pulled her up. Coll followed. On board, the deck was a flurry of

10

packing and repairing, preparing to move. Rudy stood in the centre, shouting orders, giving advice and managing the chaos. Rudy was old, and his long thick hair was white, but his eyes sparkled. He still had the best eyesight of anyone, and spent his days watching the landscape for danger or opportunities. His skin was sunburned and battered by the weather into cheerful folds. He was Beta, second in command, and had been forever. He'd never tried to be Alpha, which was probably why he was still alive.

He nodded to them. "How's pickings?"

"Coll found a tooth!" said Luna.

Rudy grinned. "Good lad." He turned back. "Luna, got a job for you, with that lot." He jerked his head towards a group of other youngsters, who were pulling on cloaks and backpacks, chattering excitedly.

"What's going on?" asked Coll.

"Oh, just checking something out," said Rudy. "No need for you to bother. Take a break, you've earned it." He sounded breezy but he looked away as he spoke.

Coll frowned. "Wait, is this a scout mission? Rudy, you said *I'd* be on the next one."

Rudy turned back. "Aye, well…" He gave an embarrassed shrug. "Sorry, lad. Orders."

Behind Rudy, a boy laughed. "No trip for you, Faulty!"

11

Rudy whipped round. "Heel!" he snapped furiously. "You use that word again, Lyall, and I'll have you clearing exhaust for a month, understand?"

The boy Lyall scowled and shuffled away. He muttered something to his friends and they snorted. Rudy rested a hand on Coll's arm, but Coll pulled away.

"Rudy, it's not fair!" he said. "She can't keep doing this!"

"Doing what?" came a voice behind him.

Coll stopped. When he turned, Alpha was gazing at him.

Alpha was long-limbed and tough, and walked with a smooth confident grace. She wasn't the strongest on board, or the fiercest, but she seemed to pulse with hidden power, as if she was holding it inside and could unleash it at any time. Her senior crew stood behind her.

"What is it that Alpha cannot do?" she asked. Her voice was calm, but its edge carried on the morning air.

Coll's face flushed. He bowed, low enough to show the back of his neck in surrender.

"Forgive me, Alpha," he muttered.

"Oh, get *up*," she snapped. Coll straightened. "Give us a moment," she said, and the others moved away. Luna gave Coll a single embarrassed smile before following Rudy. When Alpha spoke again, her voice was a little softer, but not much. "What's this about?"

Coll swallowed. "You promised me a scout trip. You said I could go, but you pulled me again!"

"It's hardly a scout trip," she said. "Rudy thought he saw something during the fight, wants to check it out, that's all."

"That's not the *point*," protested Coll. "You said I could go. You *promised*. I'm as good as the others! I can fight, I'm a good aim, I can—"

"Your arm's hurting, isn't it?" she interrupted.

Coll stopped. "What? No."

"You're rubbing it. It's hurting."

Coll scowled and forced his hand down by his side. "It's fine," he muttered.

"I just think you're not ready yet," said Alpha. "And some of the crew…" She stopped.

"Some of the crew what?"

She didn't answer, but Coll knew anyway. Some of the crew didn't trust him. Some of the crew didn't like how he was different.

Alpha sighed and looked away. "We're heading into Scatter," she said after a moment. "I'm going to talk to the mayor. You want to come with?"

Coll was still angry. He knew she was just trying to fob him off. But… He shrugged and turned away. "Fine."

"Coll." Alpha's voice was hard again. Coll clenched his fists and turned back.

"Thank you, Alpha," he said, loud enough for the others to hear. Behind him, someone sniggered. Coll's face burned. He stalked off to the side and found Rudy getting ready to leave. Luna and the others were already on the ground.

"Sorry, laddie," murmured Rudy.

"She said I could go," growled Coll. "She *promised*. She's never going to let me out of her sight!"

Rudy leapt up on to the deck rail and grabbed a tether. "You know how it is. She's just trying to protect you." He shrugged. "After all ... she *is* your mum, eh?" He stepped off.

"Have fun in Scatter!" he shouted as he disappeared down the side.

Coll watched him go. As Rudy landed, Wolf stretched her forelegs out and clambered to her feet, lifting the deck thirty metres into the air. Huge pistons drove her legs up, motors hummed, and she arched her neck.

Coll held a rope and looked at his left arm.

His own arm ended just below the elbow, and the rest was metal and plastic. His left leg was the same; the bone and muscle stopped at the knee, resting on a metal lower leg. In the morning sunlight he studied the tiny threads of anthryl that weaved in between the panels of his prosthetic lower arm and hand. They wrapped his stump in a sleeve that went up to his shoulder and across his back, holding it secure.

The anthryl powered his limb, shaped it, made it react almost as well and smoothly as his other arm. Sensors responded to his nerves, even his thoughts. Touch signals fed back to the base of his stump. He could do anything with his left arm that he could with his right. His leg was the same – he could walk, run, jump as well as anyone. It was a miracle. But still, it made him different.

And aboard Wolf, different was bad.

Down below, the figures on the ground were tiny. One, with a dash of silver hair, was Rudy, leading the others away.

Coll rubbed his arm and watched them until they were out of sight.

2

SCATTER

Scatter was just a sprawl of buildings loosely collected on the side of a hill. It was the furthest south of all the Wolf settlements; a few kilometres beyond it, the poisonous Mortal River marked the edge of the Glass Lands. No one ever entered the Glass Lands – or at least, none returned. Scatter was the edge of the liveable world.

As Wolf padded towards the town, sunshine caught on its roofs and rough streets and made them sparkle. The locals had climbed on to their flat roofs to watch, and adults and children waved at their approach.

Wolf stopped a hundred metres away from the gates. Alpha slid down a cable to the ground, followed by Dolph, the huge master-at-arms, and then Coll. They walked into town, past a sign saying:

SCATTER

UNDER WOLF

A group of officials waited for them, standing beneath a banner that read WELCOME, alongside a picture of a Wolf's head. Behind the officials were townsfolk waving little paper flags and smiling. Coll smiled back, but Alpha's face stayed serious.

The leader, Mayor Ruprecht, stepped forward. He wore an ancient black frock coat and top hat, and a silver wolf's-paw brooch on his lapel. He gave a wide smile, full of gleaming white teeth, and bowed.

"Good morning, Alpha," he said in a chuckling, oily voice. "How is Wolf today?"

Alpha glanced at the banner, the people, the flags, and then back to the mayor. She gave a tiny curt nod. "Are the supplies ready?"

The mayor clicked his fingers, and from behind them a line of wagons started to trundle down the hill, loaded with barrels and boxes, heading out to Wolf.

Alpha ignored them. "I want a report," she said.

"Of course." The mayor rubbed his hands one over the other, as if washing them. "This way." He led them through the town and the crowd cheered as they passed. Alpha walked without looking left or right.

You had to act differently in settlements. On board, Alpha was strong, fierce, but still part of the crew. But, as she had told Coll: "When you're dealing with Worms

17

you have to show them who's in charge." *Worms* were the people stuck on the ground, grubbing along in their small lives. They looked up at the Constructs, but they would never be a part of them. Coll felt a bit sorry for them.

They entered Mayor Ruprecht's offices, where the parlour had been set up ready, and sat drinking tea from tin, ancient, frail teacups. The cups were silly things that wouldn't last five minutes aboard Wolf. The first time she broke into a run they'd be smashed to pieces. Dolph held his with an expression of mild terror, as if wondering how to not crush it in his huge hands. Coll watched Alpha and tried to copy her, with her straight back and her careful, watchful face.

Mayor Ruprecht smiled at him. "You've grown again, Coll," he said. "And starting to look a lot like your mother, I reckon—"

"Report," snapped Alpha, and the man recoiled.

"It's been quiet here," he said in a suddenly business-like voice. "I understand you, ah, found Hyena?"

"Dealt with," said Alpha. She didn't add any detail, but the mayor beamed.

"Good! Good… But there are other rumours. Raven was spotted up towards Redwood. And something else, further north." He shrugged. "Just rumours."

Alpha nodded. "We're looking for anthryl – do you have any?"

The mayor gave a rumbling laugh. "Not us! We hardly see the stuff – you could buy all of Scatter with what's in there…" He nodded towards Coll's arm.

Coll pulled his sleeve down.

The mayor frowned in thought. "There's an Antoid colony a few klicks north," he said at last. "They've been hanging around, scavenging for metal, causing trouble. They might have scraps…"

"Hmm." Alpha seemed sceptical. "Show me."

The mayor brought out a map of the region, much folded and covered with old pencil marks, and pointed out the location of the colony. Alpha and Dolph studied the map. Coll studied Alpha.

Alpha didn't like it when people said Coll looked like her, or mentioned that she was his mother. And she didn't like people pointing out his prosthetics. She was supposed to be Alpha to all the crew, without favour or special treatment. But any other crew member with Coll's differences wouldn't be allowed to stay on board, and certainly wouldn't be given the resources used in his arm and leg… Coll tugged his sleeve down further, so that only the tips of his plastic fingers showed.

The discussion wore on. Now it was about details of

19

trade routes and supplies, weather reports, crops... Coll became bored. Eventually he got up and slipped outside. The mayor gave him a small nod as he left, but Alpha and Dolph didn't look up.

The banner and flags were still fluttering. It looked quite pretty, and the townsfolk smiled as he passed. Wagons were still rolling down the hill towards Wolf, where the crew loaded barrels of food, drink and material aboard. Coll wandered off the main street, exploring. Away from the centre, the town became dirty, and obviously poorer. Stone buildings with tile roofs were replaced by wooden shacks of corrugated iron. The air smelled of stale food and bad drains, and thin shoeless children peeked at him from round corners. The adults here didn't smile. They stared at him without expression.

This was the real Scatter, he knew. Away from the mayor's staff, this was life on the ground, as Worms, without shared unity or purpose. Squalid and dirty, living lives without discipline or meaning. This was why they needed Wolf – to look after them, protect them and give them purpose. Without Wolf they'd have nothing at all...

Returning to the main street, he saw a group of children on the other side of the wagons gathered in a circle. They were laughing, harsh, cruel laughter, and as

Coll watched, one of them, a girl, raised her foot and stamped, and someone screamed.

"Oink, oink!" the girl shouted. "Filthy pig, oink!"

A small shape suddenly hurtled out of the circle, raced across the road, and shot straight into the path of the wagons! Coll's breath caught in his throat, but the shape was so small it slipped right underneath, missing the wheels by a fraction. As it came out from underneath, one of the adults cursed and kicked it, and it spun.

"Run, piggy!" howled the children. "Oink, oink!"

The shape ran without looking up, smacked into Coll and bounced to the ground.

"Get him!" shouted the girl.

Coll looked down. It was a boy, winded, staring up at Coll. He was filthy. His face was a round mask of terror, and he had a shock of blond hair coated in mud. His clothes were torn and different from the other townsfolk. One hand was clenched into a fist, gripping something tight.

"What's going on?" asked Coll. He reached down and the boy tried to squirm away, back into the path of the wagons. Coll grabbed him and lifted him up. The children surrounded them. The wagons had stopped, and Coll realised the adults were watching but not intervening.

"He's a pig!" shouted the girl. "Get him!" She reached to snatch him, but Coll moved the boy away.

"What's going on?" he demanded again.

"He's a Boar runt," said Mayor Ruprecht from behind him.

Coll turned. The mayor, Alpha and Dolph had come outside. Dolph was carrying the documents they'd been discussing. Alpha said nothing, but was watching Coll carefully.

"What do you mean?" asked Coll.

The mayor shrugged. "His parents were from the Boar Construct. They came past a year ago or so. Back when we were still a Freetown, of course—" He stopped. "I mean, before we were under Wolf's *protection*, you understand." He smiled his wide oily smile. "Anyway, they'd got sick, so Boar threw them off. *You* know the rules. No sick on board Constructs, no weakness—"

For a moment, his gaze slipped to Coll's hand, then he looked away. "Erm. Well. Boar threw them off, and they made a camp out by the river."

"What happened to them?" asked Coll.

The mayor shrugged. "Who cares what happens to Boars? Died, probably." He waved an arm at the boy. "Now this runt comes into town and steals from us. Raiding our bins, getting in the way. I told the kids to

22

watch out for him. Make sure he *learns*."

Coll examined the boy. He could only be nine or so. His face was white under the mud. The girl was grinning, and her eyes gleamed with feral joy.

"We're taking him," Coll said.

Alpha's face went blank.

The mayor gaped at him in confusion. "What? Why? Why would you want—"

"Are you *questioning* us, Mayor?" asked Alpha. Her voice was quiet, but it grated like tooth on bone. Beside her, Dolph straightened and seemed to grow even larger.

The watching adults and children pulled back, and Mayor Ruprecht swallowed.

"No!" he protested. "I mean, no, not at all, take him!"

Alpha nodded. "Get these last wagons sorted," she said. "We'll take care of the Ants. Keep us informed if you hear more about these other Constructs."

She turned and stalked down the hill, ignoring Coll. Dolph followed her. Coll looked at the boy, who seemed only vaguely aware what was happening. "You come with us, OK?"

The boy said nothing, but when Coll started walking, he followed. Behind them, the children watched, glowering, but no one said anything.

No one was smiling any more.

Alpha waited until they were all the way back at Wolf before turning on Coll.

"What in the name of the moon did you think you were doing?" she snapped. Her eyes flashed with fury.

Coll stepped back. "They were attacking him!" he said hotly. "I had to do something!" Beside him, the little boy shrank under Alpha's anger.

"*Why?*" she demanded. "What do we care what they do with some *pig* brat? You think we've got space to hold it? Food to feed it?"

"Then why didn't you say so back there?"

Dolph rolled his eyes. Alpha stared at Coll. "We are *Wolf*," she said at last in an icy voice. "When we are on the ground, when we go into these places, we are one. We *speak* as one. If you admit weakness, your allies will turn on you, your enemies will strike. We don't show indecision, we don't reveal personal feelings, and we don't *argue* in front of the *Worms!*"

Coll swallowed. "I'm sorry," he said quietly. "He's just a child, Alpha."

She scowled. "Well, that *child* is your problem now."

"What, me?" he asked, confused.

"Yes, you! You brought it here, so now you look after it. Feed it, clothe it…" She shook her head. "And clean up after its mess."

Alpha grabbed a cable and tugged, and it lifted her up. Behind her, Dolph chuckled and tugged on another cable.

"Remember to feed it every day," he called as he disappeared up the side.

Coll looked down at the boy.

"Well," he said weakly, "I suppose you'd better come with me."

3

FiLLAN

The boy at least seemed to remember how to get on board. He held on to a cable and let it pull him up, and Coll followed him. As they came over the deck rail, some of the crew turned and stared.

"This way," muttered Coll. The boy followed slowly, gazing at everything – the metal beams, the entranceway, the Wolf crew. He was blinking a lot and clutching tight to a little leather bag.

"They said you were on Boar," said Coll. The boy gave a vague nod. "You remember it?" He shrugged. Coll realised he hadn't heard him say a single word.

"What's your name?"

At first he didn't answer. Then he muttered, "F-Farrow." His voice creaked as if rusty.

"Farrow?" Coll shook his head. "What's that, a pig name? Come on, through here. Hurry up. That's not a proper name. You need something Wolf. Like … I don't know. Fillan. That means 'little wolf'. You're Fillan now, OK?"

The boy looked at him. "OK," he whispered.

"This way," said Coll. "Watch the step. Watch the *step*—"

The boy tumbled forward and landed hard on the metal floor with an "*Oof!*"

Coll cursed. "I told you to watch!" he snapped. "You all right?"

The boy sat up. One hand was scraped where he'd tried to stop himself from falling. He hadn't let go of the bag. His face was red. He nodded.

"Come on," said Coll, and hoisted him to his feet. "You're OK."

"OK," the boy echoed. Then he turned in the direction of the galley and the smell of food.

"You hungry?" asked Coll.

The boy said nothing, but his face looked pinched and his stomach suddenly gave a huge growl.

Coll nodded. "Food first."

It was quiet, between shifts. Coll brought him some stew. He thought the boy would have disgusting manners, like everyone knew Boars had, but he ate quickly and neatly, keeping one hand curled tight round his bowl

27

and scraping it clean. Coll brought him another bowl, and another, and at last the boy slowed.

"You done?" asked Coll.

The boy nodded. His eyes were glazed, as if half asleep.

"Come on, then." Coll led him out.

As they left, Farkas the cook laughed. "Got yourself a little pet piglet, eh?" he said.

Coll shook his head and scowled.

"Here," he said, leading the boy through to a dorm room. "This is our den."

The boy looked around. The room was small, just enough for ten sets of bunks. Coll said, "You'll sleep here with us kids. When we're fourteen we go with the bigger kids."

The boy sat on a bunk.

"Not that one!" snapped Coll. The boy jumped as if stung. "Look, *here*." He led him to one corner. "The top bunk is mine. You can have the bottom one."

The boy sat on the bottom bunk. "On Boar we could sleep anywhere," he said in a small voice.

"Boars are stupid and filthy and bathe in mud," replied Coll. "On Wolf we do things right. *This* is your bunk. Nowhere else, understand?"

The boy nodded. Coll hesitated. He wasn't sure how

he expected the child to behave. He said, "There's a shelf here. Anything you put there is safe – no one will touch it."

The boy looked at it, and then down at his hand, still clutching the little bag. He didn't move.

Coll frowned. "What's in there, anyway?"

The boy gripped the bag tighter.

Coll raised his hands. "I won't *take* it."

The boy stared at him and bit his lip. Then he tipped the bag out on to his bunk. There was a little wooden boar's head, and three water-smoothed pebbles, grey with swirling white, two large and one small.

"What are they?" asked Coll. He reached for one, but the boy clutched them. Coll pulled back. "It's fine, really. Is it a game?" But they didn't seem like game pieces. And there was something about the way he held them so tight… "What are they, then?"

The boy didn't answer. He arranged the two larger pebbles on the bunk. He placed the smaller pebble between them and stared at them. It didn't make sense to Coll, at first. Then he thought they looked like a little family. One baby pebble and two parents…

"Oh," he said, finally understanding. Water dripped on to them, and he realised tears were rolling down the boy's cheeks. He felt a sudden horrified panic. "Don't cry!" he said in alarm.

The boy recoiled as if he thought Coll was going to hit him. His chest heaved with sobs, though he made no sound. Coll had no idea what to do. Rudy was away. Should he get Alpha? Farkas? *Dolph?* Anyone! "It's all right!" he tried. "Well, no, it isn't, but … but…"

He patted the boy's shoulder awkwardly, then sat next to him on the bunk.

He sighed. "I'm sorry," he said softly. "I suppose you've had a rough time."

The boy didn't answer.

Coll said, "I don't know what happened. Happened before, I mean. But, look, that's … that's you *before*. It's all right now. OK? So you can stop crying. Stop crying now."

It didn't seem to work. Coll had an idea. "Hey, look." He reached round his neck and unfastened a chain. It held a small wooden carving of a wolf, and Coll showed it to the boy. "We are Wolf, understand?" Carefully he reached for the little boar's head. The boy stiffened but said nothing, and Coll took the boar's head and gave him the wolf chain instead.

"You're with us now," he said. "See? You're *Fillan* now. You are Wolf. *We* are Wolf. We'll look after you. Everything will be all right."

The little boy sniffed and nodded. Gradually his chest

stopped heaving. He nodded again. Then he suddenly wrapped his arms round Coll and gripped him in a fierce tight hug, pressing his damp face against Coll's chest.

"Oh!" exclaimed Coll. "Um…" He patted the boy on the back, then prised him away and stood up, embarrassed. "Well," he said gruffly, "yes, OK. Come on, I can't hang around here all day."

The boy Fillan put the pebbles back in his bag. He still held the bag tight, but he'd stopped crying. He looked up at Coll, sniffed and half smiled. "OK."

Coll showed him where to wash and got him some new clothes to replace his filthy old Boar outfit. He seemed to like his new grey-black cloak, running his hands down it. Then Coll led him back to his bunk and he crept under the covers.

"Get some sleep," said Coll, and turned to leave.

"Don't go!" said Fillan, sounding scared again.

"I've got duties," protested Coll. "I can't spend all my time here with you."

"Don't go."

Coll scowled. "One minute." He sat on Fillan's bunk. "That's all, OK?"

"OK."

Fillan closed his eyes. One hand reached out and found Coll's and patted it. Coll sat, wondering what to do, but before the minute was up, Fillan's breathing had deepened, and he was asleep. Coll crept out.

That evening, when everyone came to bed, Fillan was snoring. He was still holding tight to his little leather bag.

Coll climbed into his own bunk. He unclipped his leg and arm, sighing in relief as they came away, and rubbed the base of his stumps. Then he tucked the prosthetics on his shelf, lay back, and stared at the roof of the den, wondering what he had done.

When he awoke the next morning, Wolf was on the move, and the room was swaying around him. He remembered Fillan and peered down into the bottom bunk. The boy was awake, looking up.

"Hey," said Coll.

Fillan smiled at him. "Hey," he whispered.

Coll fastened his prosthetics back on and pulled his sleeve down before swinging out of his bunk. "Come on," he said, yawning. "Let's see what's going on."

Dolph was on deck. He glanced at them and grinned. "Still alive, little pig?" he called to Fillan. "Well done! Ready for some hunting?"

"Where are we going?" asked Coll.

"Helping the mayor with his Ant problem. See if we can salvage some anthryl."

Rudy's scout team were still out, so Wolf stopped on the top of a hill, visible from a long way off, so they could find her when they returned. Dolph arranged the crew into groups and pointed westwards, towards a small wood a kilometre away. The wood was surrounded by long sandy-coloured grass, and Coll could make out faint tracks as if someone had walked back and forth there.

"Keep in pairs," said Dolph. He handed them each a zapper. "If you get in trouble, then holler."

Fillan examined the zapper: a short grey tube with a handle. "What's this?"

"It fires a charge that disables the Ants," said Coll.

Fillan held his up and peered down the barrel.

Coll sighed, took it off him, and handed it back to Dolph. "Let's … just use mine today."

"OK."

They headed out through the long pale grass, Fillan half trotting beside Coll. Fed, washed and in his new cloak, he seemed remarkably recovered, though he stayed next to Coll at all times. He was wearing Coll's chain and had fastened his little bag to it.

"What are we doing?" he asked.

"Hunting Ants. Antoids," said Coll. "Have you done that before?"

Fillan shook his head.

33

Coll shrugged. "It's easy. Just don't let them surround you." He pointed towards the wood. "That's probably the nest."

"But why—"

"Shh." Coll stopped. Up ahead, there was a rustling sound, and a metallic *clat-clat-clat*. There was a smell in the air like copper. He crept forward and peered through the grass.

A line of Ants walked along the trail.

They were a mix of colours: some steel, some rust red, some bright, depending on what they were made of. They looked roughly like insects, with six legs, a thorax and round heads with long antennae. But the thorax was a power supply, and the legs were articulated metal, and the 'eyes' were scanners. They were each a metre long and about as tall as Coll's knees.

Coll pulled back. He waited until the line had almost passed, and then carefully threw a stone at the Ant third from the end. It hit with a soft *dink* and the Ant stopped. It looked at the stone, then lifted its head and moved it this way and that. Its mandibles slid over each other, as if thinking, making a sound. "Chick-chick?" it seemed to ask. "Chick-chick?"

It turned and left the path, pushing through the long grass. The two Ants behind it followed. "Chick-chick?"

asked the one at the back.

"Chick-chick," said the near one.

Coll waited until all three had walked into the grass, then lifted his zapper and fired, one-two-three, and the Ants' metal bodies collapsed. One tipped over on to its back and lay with its legs in the air. Coll checked them carefully before lowering his zapper.

"There," he said to Fillan. "Easy, see? You just have to make sure they don't swarm you." He fetched some rope from his bag and tied them together. "Three's enough for one run."

As they heaved them back towards Wolf, Fillan asked, "Where do the Ants come from?"

"All over," said Coll. "They make a nest and forage for scrap materials. Then they use it to make new Ants. They use metal, plastic, even wood sometimes." He grinned as he remembered the night-time horror stories the older children liked to tell. "Sometimes old *bones*…"

But Fillan shook his head. "I mean, where did they come from to begin with?"

"No idea." Coll shrugged. "Old times. I guess someone made the first ones. They've got anthryl in them, like Wolf, just a bit. The Tocks will scrape it out."

They left the meadow. Wolf was up ahead, and Coll could see activity around her, buzzing and urgent.

35

Someone ran towards them, waving, and he recognised Luna, back from the scout trip. He waved back.

"Coll!" she shouted. "Leave that! Come on!"

Fillan pulled back behind Coll. Luna glanced at him and frowned in surprise, but then ignored him. "We found a supply cache!" she said.

She raced back towards Wolf, and Coll and Fillan ran to keep up. "What's the rush?" panted Coll.

Luna grinned a hard, fierce grin. "Not just us," she said. "Raven found it too. Come on!"

4

THE CALL

Coll and Fillan scrambled up on deck after Luna, as Wolf prepared for battle.

The crew was getting ready to move, tying down equipment and barrels, checking harnesses, and Alpha and the senior crew were standing at the head deck. And under his feet, Coll could feel Wolf's excitement, her hackles about to rise, that thrum and whisper of her Call.

"We found it on the third day," chattered Luna in an excited voice. "The wind must have uncovered it. It's a full cache, just waiting there, doesn't seem to be disturbed or anything!" But then she saw Coll's face, and she grimaced. "Sorry. I wish you could have come with us."

Behind her, Lyall pushed past with his friends. "Yeah, shame you weren't there, eh?" he called in a mocking voice. "Still. Wasn't anyone's … *fault*."

Coll stepped forward, but suddenly Rudy was at his

side. The old man's face was friendly, but his hand gripped Coll's arm like iron. "Steady," he murmured.

Lyall chuckled and swaggered away. He would share the glory, Coll knew, just for being part of the scout group. Finding a *cache*…

"What's a cache?" asked Fillan.

Rudy looked down at the boy and grinned. "Ah, Alpha told me about *you*," he said. He crouched down to Fillan's height. "A little piglet come to join our crew, is it? What's your name, lad?"

Fillan looked at him but said nothing. He tucked himself slightly behind Coll.

"It's Fillan," said Coll. "He's Wolf now."

Rudy nodded. "Good to have you aboard, young Fillan," he said. "Alpha tells me Coll recruited you all by himself…" His eyes crinkled. "Now, what would make him do that, I wonder?"

Coll shrugged, embarrassed. "I just…" he said, and stopped. "He was in trouble. He needed someone to look after him."

"Too soft for your own good, you are," said Rudy, but he was smiling. He turned back to Fillan. "A cache, lad, is a stack of supplies. Something left ages ago, by the old folks. Fuel, equipment, weapons, water, anthryl for repairs … *everything*. A cache is *gold*." He stood straight and kept talking while he watched the crew prepare. "We found it by chance, headed back right away. But then Raven saw *us*. We hid in the forest and escaped her, but she's out there. And she'll have figured out what we were looking for."

"Why's Raven even here?" asked Coll.

Rudy nodded. "Good question. It's not like her to leave her territory. And Hyena before her..." His lips pursed. "There must be something going on up north, pushing them south—" He broke off to shout at a crew member fastening a canister, then turned back and nodded towards Fillan. "You'd better get the whelp strapped in. Luna, help below. Hoy! Mingan, get that rope cleared away, you lazy cur!"

He strode off, and Coll led Fillan to a seat near the middle of the deck, strapping him in tight and attaching his tether. Around him, the crew were doing the same, or clearing the last of the loose equipment on board. Below decks, he knew the galley would be hurriedly stowing pans and plates. Tocks ran past, holding scanners and talking in their fast half-gibberish, while ahead, Alpha, Dolph and Rudy took their positions.

"What's going on?" asked Fillan nervously, but Coll didn't answer. He was looking across at the Tock girl Rieka, working at a panel near one of the storage bins tailside. Everyone else was rushing around, but she was standing still, with her back to the chaos. She was carrying a leather pack bag, and as Coll watched, she glanced about, quickly slipped the storage bin open, removed three wrapped packets and stuffed them into her bag. She did it in a single movement before returning to the control panel – it happened so fast Coll almost thought he'd imagined it.

She walked off to the next panel as if nothing had happened. Coll frowned. What could she have been doing? Why take those packets? She'd looked shifty, but there was nothing in that bin but rations and food supplies. And there was plenty of food aboard after their trip to Scatter, enough for all the crew. He stared as she moved to the next panel.

"Coll!" Coll looked down. Fillan was tugging at his shirt. The little boy looked nervous. "What's going on?"

Coll shook his head. "We're on the move," he said. "Do you know what you have to do? The Call, I mean. Do you know how to respond to the Call? Did you do that on Boar?"

Fillan gaped at him. "They said I was too small," he said.

Coll scowled. "They taught you *nothing*," he muttered.

"You're big enough. All right. Just … listen. Listen to the deck."

Fillan looked at him and then at the deck. "What?"

"Shh. Listen through your feet. You can feel it move, right?" Fillan nodded. "Now, listen further. Under the movement, there's a sound. Hear it with your feet." Coll heard it himself. The soft, steady, deep, strong beat that surrounded them, protected them, guided them. "You hear it? Like a heartbeat. Like a song."

As he spoke, Coll let his attention drift down into the deck. He ignored the people rushing around them, and the sounds of shouting and orders. He felt the pistons moving underneath, and the hum of motors. He felt all the parts of the great machine preparing to run, and the silver blood running through huge veins, leading to the very centre of Wolf. The way everything worked together. The heart…

Coll felt the Call.

Suddenly he wasn't hearing Wolf, or feeling her. He *was* her, alongside all the rest of the crew – Alpha, Rudy, Luna, Rieka and the other Tocks, even Lyall and his mates. They were all part of one single creature. They thought together as Wolf. Their hearts beat together.

We are Wolf.

And now there was a new tiny flickering heartbeat,

and he knew that Fillan had joined them. And Fillan was Wolf too – albeit a slightly round wolf, with thick black hairs like a boar…

Coll opened his eyes. Fillan was staring at him. "Oh!" the boy said, and Coll smiled.

"This is what it means to be Wolf," he murmured. "This is the Call. When we fight, we all fight. We are Wolf. You understand?" Fillan nodded, but Coll persisted. "*We are Wolf*. There is *only* Wolf. Nothing else matters. Nothing else *exists*. Understand?" Fillan nodded again.

Coll grinned. "Well done."

Fillan smiled at him, and for a moment Coll felt oddly proud.

"Rudy, what's our status?" bellowed Alpha.

"Last ones coming aboard now!" called Rudy. Two men found a place and strapped in. "All set!"

"Wolf!" shouted Alpha.

"WOLF!" roared the crew.

And beneath them the huge Construct's head lifted, and her teeth bared, and she ran.

She ran from a standing start, her massive back legs driving her forward, her forelegs stretching out, gripping the ground. The deck pitched and rolled as she ran. Stabilisers squealed and gyroscopes kept them as level as possible, but still the crew swung up and down in their seats. It was wild and chaotic and exhilarating. Coll could feel his body on deck, shaking back and forth – but from a distance somehow, as if watching. He was Wolf now. Wolf was him. It was *his* legs running, *his* heart pounding, *his* tongue lolling from an open mouth, feeling the air rushing past.

The part of him that was still Coll looked down at Fillan. "YOU OK?"

The boy was white-faced but he raised one shaky thumb and gave a half-smile.

Coll laughed. "Isn't she wonderful?" he roared.

All around him he felt the love of Wolf's crew, the beat of their hearts. Arguments didn't matter any more. Only Wolf mattered. Their belief was the energy that drove Wolf on.

Wolf ran, her crew ran, she was the pack, and the pack was strong!

She bounded across the land with her huge strides, eating up the kilometres, feeling the wind against her face. Through a patch of long grass, leaping over a river, racing between two small hills and out over the plain. At her head, Rudy pointed, and Coll could make out something glinting in the sun – a metal doorway seeming to rise out of the grass, half covered by a large fallen tree.

Wolf saw it too with a fierce joy that rippled through the crew. But then she saw something else on the far side. Danger. An enemy. An *intruder*.

It was black, with massive wings that shimmered with metallic iridescence, the sun catching on its feathers. It had a long grey beak and it was dark grey round its neck, with more feathers that seemed to puff up around it. Its wings were beating in powerful swings. It was almost as large as Wolf, and already it was close enough for Coll to make out a deck and perhaps even tiny people on board…

Raven.

"Prepare for battle!" shouted Alpha. "Rudy, ready the net!" Beside her, two Tocks jabbed at their control panels. Wolf edged closer, and the huge bird swooped and turned towards them. Wolf gave a slavering growl and they heard an answering shrieking *CAW!* from the enemy.

"Hold fast!" shouted Alpha. "WOLF! WOLF!"

Wolf *leapt*.

5

RAVEN

Wolf's hind legs bunched and thrust her up into a huge leap, as high as Raven, catching the enemy Construct by surprise. Her mouth was open wide and she snapped her jaws hard enough to crack Raven's head.

"*WOLF!*" roared her crew.

But Raven was fast. Her wings bent as she reared back, and Wolf missed her by a metre. As she landed, Raven swooped down and stabbed with her beak. Wolf turned and the beak glanced against her shoulder. Wolf snapped at her, but she pulled herself up with awkward wingbeats and away.

Coll scowled. That first leap had been their best chance. From now on Raven could stay out of reach, swooping and stabbing. Wolf would have to endure it and try to counterattack. Coll felt the crew realise the same thing, and their faith dimmed a little.

"WOLF!" he bellowed. Beside him, Fillan squeaked, "Wolf!"

Raven came in low and fast, staying clear of Wolf's jaws, and stabbed again, twisting at the last moment. Her razor-sharp beak smashed through Wolf's side panels and carved into the deck with a sickening crunch. Crew members scattered and fled, and equipment shuddered loose.

"No!" shouted Fillan. But Wolf was sly. She didn't shy away, but leaned *in*, and then tumbled in a roll. Raven's beak was tangled in the wreckage of the deck, and she was carried along with Wolf. The deck heaved, turning all the way over, and Coll felt the chair straps dig into his shoulders. Now all Wolf's weight came down hard on Raven and she gave a startled squawk. For a second, Coll could see Raven's crew *underneath* them, staring up in horror as Wolf threatened to break their back.

Raven scrambled away, her claws raking at Wolf, her beak heaving as she tried to untangle herself. She managed, but her wings flapped raggedly.

"WOOOOOOLF!" roared Wolf's crew, and Coll felt their energy again, their belief.

Wolf turned and leapt again!

And missed. Raven wasn't as hurt as she'd pretended – it had been a feint, and now she swooped down. Again

46

that horrible beak stabbed once, twice, three times against Wolf. Now she dived at Wolf's head, aiming for her eyes!

"Net!" shouted Alpha. Her voice cut through the chaos, fierce but not afraid. Men and women jumped from their harnesses and ran to the sides, heaving a huge black net from its container.

"Come on!" roared Coll. He dragged Fillan to the side to join the adults. He looked down at the boy. "Are you tethered?" Fillan nodded. "Good!" shouted Coll. "Help with the net!"

Wolf started to roll again, and Coll's heart lurched. He grabbed Fillan. But it was a ruse; Raven squawked in panic and pulled away, and Wolf *lunged*. Her jaws closed round the tip of Raven's wing, ripping at metal feathers. Raven cawed in pain. Wolf turned away, presenting her flank to the great bird. An easy target… Raven swooped in.

"Now!" shouted Alpha. As one, the crew cast the net out, and roared as Raven became tangled. She shrieked and tried to pull free.

"Hold!" bellowed Alpha. Coll could see Raven's crew scattering in panic. "Hold!"

Coll hauled at the net with all his might. Here was what he loved, in the thick of the fighting. He was still young, but tall for his age and proud of his strength. His muscles rippled as he pulled, and he realised the adults next to him were following *his* rhythm. *Heave. Heave.* He glanced across at Alpha, hoping she could see him at this moment, but she was talking with the Tocks. The Tocks looked worried. Wolf had been hurt by that stabbing beak. Everything depended on holding Raven trapped like this.

"Heave!" he roared, and the adults roared with him. "Heave!"

Raven shrieked and fluttered her wings, desperate to get away.

Coll's arm ached with an unpleasant twang, but he ignored it and pulled again and again. Raven was tiring, he could tell! "Heave! Heave! Heave——"

Then he felt his left arm *wrench*.

Something happened inside the arm, and the motors inside it spun wild and then jerked. A silver-blue arc of lightning flickered up the sleeve and into his shoulder and he yelped in pain. Then, with no control of his own, his left hand released the net.

"No!" he roared. He stumbled and tripped against the man beside him, and the man cursed and toppled over, releasing the net. The line faltered and lost their rhythm. On Coll's other side, Fillan stared down at him. Coll scrambled to his feet and grabbed the net with his right arm.

"Keep pulling!" he shouted, but it was too late. Raven, feeling the tension ease, gave a huge heave backwards and scraped loose. She left behind black feathers, but she was free, and she cawed in ferocious joy. Coll could hear her crew cheering.

She climbed high into the air and attacked again, keeping the sun behind her.

Rudy and the Tocks were shouting something to Alpha. Wolf was weak and injured. Alpha's face was like stone. She stared at the oncoming Construct for one second, two...

"Heel!" she roared. "Fall back!"

Wolf shook her head and stumbled away. She kept her jaws open and facing Raven, but she moved back a step and another. Raven swooped and stabbed and drove at Wolf, and Coll sagged as he felt Wolf's power fade.

Raven's crew were roaring in delight. "RAVEN! RAVEN! CAW, CAW, CAW!"

Wolf gave one final snarl and retreated, and the two metal beasts faced each other a hundred metres apart. Raven was damaged. She settled on the ground, one wing tattered and torn. It was stalemate. Neither of them could turn their back on the other.

"Damage report, Dolph," said Alpha. Her voice gave no hint of defeat. "Rudy, see to the net. Everyone, we'll take a break once the net's in, then you can rest and eat."

And only now did she turn and look at Coll – at the dead metal of his arm, and the circle around him where the others had moved away.

She sighed. "Coll … go and see the Tocks."

They waited in the medical bay, Coll and Fillan. Fillan had followed Coll without asking, and now he sat on the bed next to him, staring. They said nothing. After a few minutes, Fillan tentatively reached out as if about to poke at Coll's arm.

"*Don't*," snapped Coll.

Fillan pulled his hand back. He frowned. "What's wrong with it?" he asked.

Coll closed his eyes. "I don't know."

"Does it hurt?"

It was agony. It was like someone had pulled his arm up behind his back hard enough to heave it out of its socket. His stump pulsed with hot pain like a scream.

"No," he said.

The door opened. Intrick, the dour old Tock, entered, scratching his chin. Behind him was Rieka. Intrick looked up at Coll and scowled.

"Oh, it's you," he said in a disgruntled voice. He glanced at Coll's arm. "During the fight?" he asked. Coll nodded, and Intrick turned to Rieka. "Inspect it."

Rieka stepped forward and examined Coll's arm. She unfolded a small set of screwdrivers and poked at it.

"Rupture at the second junction," she muttered. "Fused across."

"Is that bad?" asked Coll nervously.

The girl ignored him. "Three points down," she said. As she moved the screwdriver inside the arm, he felt ripples of sensation against his stump; not painful, but strange and *wrong*. He twitched.

"Stay still," she ordered. He clenched his jaw and said nothing.

"Restarting…" she muttered. "Booting sequence…"

The arm spasmed, and then Coll felt it reconnect. Suddenly he had two arms again, and he breathed out in relief. The sharp pain became a low ache as his shoulder relaxed.

The girl stepped back. "That's it."

Intrick nodded. "Good." He turned to leave.

"What happened?" asked Coll.

Intrick turned back. He didn't answer at first, and when he did speak, it was as if he was talking to the room.

"Wolf is our home," he intoned. "Wolf is our *world*.

51

We belong to her. We have *faith* in her. Where there is faith, there is health. Where there is faith, we are as one. But where our faith is weak…" He glanced at Coll and shrugged.

"I'm not weak!" protested Coll. "I have faith. I believe in Wolf. I *do*."

"You argued with Alpha," said the old man triumphantly. "You questioned her orders!"

Coll didn't answer, and Intrick nodded. He gestured towards Coll's metal arm and leg. "This flaw is *your fault*, Coll. Because your faith is weak. Alpha may choose to ignore it, for whatever reason…" He let that hang in the air. They both knew the reason. "But only Wolf matters. Think on that. Find your *faith*, and Wolf will make you whole."

He smiled, and then glanced at Fillan. His lip curled. "Check the pig boy for disease," he said, and turned and left.

Rieka picked up her scanner and pointed it at Fillan.

Fillan watched her for a few seconds. Then he said to Coll, "Is this why the others call you Faulty?"

"Who said that?" snarled Coll, and Fillan recoiled. Coll rubbed his hand over his face. "Sorry. Yes. Yes, Fillan. Of course that's why."

Rieka snapped her scanner closed. "You're fine," she

52

said to Fillan. She turned to Coll. "Your arm will be fine too."

Coll sighed. "Yes, I know, if I consider my faith."

Rieka rolled her eyes. "Don't be stupid," she said. "There's a weak point in the extensor tendon module. If you twist it during exertion it can trip the signal and short out. I've reset it." She shook her head. "'Faith'. Stupid."

She left without looking back.

Coll and Fillan stared after her.

"What did that mean?" asked Fillan after a moment.

Coll felt his elbow. "I don't know," he said slowly. He shook his head. "Come on, we'd better go and help with repairs."

When they came on deck, the atmosphere was strange. A few of the crew looked at Coll as he arrived, and their mouths twisted when they saw his arm. He pulled his sleeve down. But it wasn't just that. Repair teams were working all over the deck, applying anthryl patches and steel braces to fix the worst of the damage, but they were moving even faster than usual, running from place to place. At the head deck, the senior crew spoke in urgent tones.

He saw Luna dragging barrels away from a damaged area. "Luna, what's happening?" he asked. "Is it Raven?

Is Raven moving?"

Luna shook her head. "Not Raven." She pointed over the side to the north-east.

Gazing out, Coll saw a shimmer on the horizon. It was too small to make out properly, but he knew what it meant.

"What is it?" asked Fillan, peering.

Coll swallowed. "It's *another* Construct."

6

THE CACHE

Coll and Fillan worked with the others, repairing Wolf, heaving and fetching. The atmosphere was tense, and the crew looked up often – at Raven, still nearby, and at the dot on the horizon. The new Construct was still too far away to identify, but coming closer.

As he worked, Coll thought about Rieka and her strange comments. He'd heard Intrick's sermon before. He had faith in Wolf – he did. He *believed* in Wolf. He believed in Alpha…

Stupid, Rieka had called it. What had she meant?

"Coll?"

Coll looked down, and Fillan pointed.

"Should we go?"

Coll realised Alpha was standing at the head deck, ready to talk to the crew. He nodded, and he and Fillan joined the others.

"Wolf," said Alpha in a clear, strong voice. Her face was calm.

"Wolf," echoed the crew. They were united but low, and Alpha nodded.

"It's been a hard few days," she said. "Our fight with Hyena was glorious but with little reward. And Raven is still out there."

There was silence. Then a voice muttered, "Yeah, and we know why, eh?" A few of the crew glanced at Coll and he felt his face go red.

Alpha stiffened. "Something you want to say, Mingan?"

The crowd opened round the man. He scowled. "Kid lost the net, Alpha," he said. "Lost our chance, him and that arm of his – you saw it!"

Alpha didn't answer. Coll stared down at the deck, hardly breathing.

"*I* saw," said Rudy suddenly. "I saw *you*, Mingan, cowering in your seat while Coll ran for the net. I saw him pulling harder than half of you. That *kid* was showing you what it means to be Wolf!"

Coll looked up in surprise. There was steel in Rudy's voice, and Mingan seemed startled.

Then Rudy laughed. "What happened, you get tangled up in your harness again?" The crowd laughed too, and Mingan subsided, his face dark with anger.

56

Alpha nodded. She still hadn't looked at Coll. "We're here now," she said. "And we have a new guest." She pointed over the side to the dot on the horizon.

"Who is it?" asked Luna.

Alpha turned to Rudy, who nodded. "Bit far away to be sure," he said. "But I reckon it looks like Dragon."

There was a pause. Then someone in the crowd sniggered. "*Dragon?*" They turned to each other and grinned.

Fillan whispered, "Who's Dragon?"

"An old Construct," muttered Coll. "Very weak."

He shook his head. *Dragon?* He'd only ever seen it once before. They'd fought, though it had hardly been a real fight. Dragon was a silly creature, bright green and gold, with a round body and stubby wings that could hardly lift it. Mostly it only ever used them to fly away from danger. It had no real territory, no settlements under it. Rumour was it had eventually collapsed and been abandoned.

Rudy grinned. "Yeah. I don't think we need to worry too much about them."

But Alpha looked more serious. "Dragon is from the north. Hyena and Raven are from the north. None of them are strong enough to think they could take Wolf territory, but they came anyway. Something is driving them south."

The crew grew quiet. Alpha pointed towards the strange metal doorway of the cache a few hundred metres away.

"That's a supply cache there, and we need it. We're low on anthryl and equipment for the Tocks, things we can't get from the settlements. Raven wants them too." She spoke with authority. "We can take Raven. And Dragon could never be a match for us. But fighting both will be hard." She gazed round the crew and grinned. "But we are *Wolf*. We are strong, we are fierce ... and we are *cunning*.

"So here is what we are going to do."

Dragon arrived an hour later. It wasn't as brightly coloured as Coll remembered – some of the green and gold seemed weather-worn and patched and had been repaired with dull grey plates. But the wings were the same, webbed like a bat, and the long neck and wide flaring nostrils. It looked ridiculous, but it took up position as if ready for a fight. The three Constructs stood in a triangle around the cache, each watching the other two.

"Why's it here?" asked Fillan, staring at it.

Coll shook his head. "Don't know. It must have guessed there was a cache. Or it's been driven down like the others, like Alpha said. Come on, give me a hand here."

Wolf had turned sideways to Raven, and now her crew were busy bringing equipment down on the hidden side – nets, pulleys, wagons, barrels and containers, all stealthily lowered to the ground. The crew worked quickly and quietly under Dolph's orders. The sun was low on the horizon and they would have to be fast.

Last to come were enormous groundsheets, mottled and painted the same colours as the landscape, covering the equipment. Rudy looked down from Wolf's deck and nodded. Then the groundcrew, including Coll, Fillan, Luna and Lyall, crawled behind the piles and laid low.

Half the crew stayed on board. It was a risk – if Raven or Dragon attacked now, the groundcrew would be defenceless and Wolf wouldn't be at full strength.

The sun sank over the horizon and the moon came out, partially covered by thick clouds. As they waited, a drizzle began to fall. The air felt thick, as if waiting for a thunderstorm.

When it was almost dark, Wolf started to move.

She padded towards Raven, steady and grim. Coll felt the ground tremble as she stepped. At first, Raven didn't react, but then she hopped a little distance away. Her wings flapped as if preparing to fly. Wolf moved round in a circle and Raven turned to watch. But she couldn't go too far, for fear of turning her back on Dragon. She had to move away from the cache.

Coll held his breath. If Raven attacked, she would discover how weak Wolf really was. But Wolf was careful. She came close but not too close. Threatening but not attacking. And gradually she manoeuvred Raven away.

"Now," whispered Dolph, and the groundcrew crept forward. They dragged the wagons and pallets towards the cache, moving the groundsheets as they did. Wolf danced her careful slow waltz with Raven, keeping her attention. Behind Raven, Dragon moved too.

Coll and the others inched towards the cache entrance. Coll could see it clearly now – a tall square-topped doorway poking out of the ground, made of silver steel that gleamed in the moonlight. Weeds and vines covered it, under the remains of an enormous tree that had been struck by lightning. The tree must have kept it hidden all these years.

Intrick stepped up to the doorway, holding a small device. He held it up and a panel on the door lit up, and then the door slid open. Caches were ancient, hundreds of years old, but the door hardly made a sound.

Dolph turned to the others. "Come on," he whispered.

They pulled their wagons forward, through the doorway and into a long tunnel sloping downwards. The tunnel had a high ceiling and perfectly smooth metal walls; the floor was black and shiny. Tiny red lights glowed every two metres. Fillan stared at everything with his mouth open, and Coll had to poke him to get him to move. But he wanted to stare too – he'd never seen a cache, only heard stories.

"Hurry," urged Dolph, pushing them on. At the far end the tunnel opened out into wide entrance, with a sign hanging above it.

UNITY SUPPLY CACHE #35 it read. Underneath was a picture of a settlement, but like no settlement Coll had ever seen. The houses in this picture were gleaming blocks with tall clear windows and grass and flowers in front. Families stood next to each house, waving and smiling. They didn't look like settlement folk either. Their clothes were strange but clean and brightly coloured. Their teeth seemed to glow white.

"Who are they?" whispered Fillan.

Coll shrugged. If they were living on the ground, they had to be Worms, so who cared? Below the picture were the words COLONY INC. – WE MAKE YOUR WORLD™.

Dolph turned to them. "Critical items only, remember. Anthryl and whatever the Tocks tell you. Nothing else, understand?"

He walked past the sign and the groundcrew followed.

61

As they turned the corner, Coll and Fillan stopped in amazement.

Ahead of them was a vast storage room stretching away in every direction. Shelves ran the length of it, two metres high, loaded with reels of cable, containers, machinery, tools … *everything*.

"Whoa," murmured Fillan, and Coll nodded.

"Let's get started," said Dolph.

7

DRAGON

Coll and Fillan got to work, dragging out crates and tubes. The Tocks pointed them towards shelves and shelves of stock. There was so much! And they could take so little! Reels of anthryl went in the wagon, lengths of good steel, and Tock equipment too, strange green boards and things with lots of wiring, more and more of it, until finally Dolph stepped in.

"Is this *all* critical?" he asked one.

She looked down at the box in her hands and her shoulders slumped and she put it back.

Dolph nodded. "That's everything!" he called. "Quickly now, out!"

They moved the wagons out of the warehouse and up the tunnel.

"Stay quiet," murmured Dolph. "We don't know how far away they'll be, and the sound carries."

They made it outside. Intrick used his device to close the door again and the lights went dim.

Coll peered out into the night. It was dark – the sun was down and the moon was half hidden by clouds. The rain was getting harder and turning the ground to mud. In the distance Wolf was a shimmer of grey facing Raven. Raven was flying now, preparing for attack, still trying to keep both Wolf and Dragon in sight. Dragon had moved too – it had turned, watching the other two.

This was the most dangerous moment, as they loaded everything on to Wolf. The groundcrew were still vulnerable, Wolf's defences would be down and Raven was alert and ready to attack. They needed a distraction. Beside them, Intrick held his device up to his ear and Coll thought he could hear Alpha's voice coming from it. Intrick spoke into the device, listened some more, then nodded to Dolph.

"Be ready," murmured Dolph.

Up ahead, Wolf took a sudden swift step towards Raven. Raven reared back, flapping her wings furiously. Wolf pulled back, then advanced again, and Raven pulled back again. Even from here, Coll could sense Raven's confusion. What was Wolf doing? One more step forward. And then again, sharp and furious, and Raven pulled back once more…

Then Dragon attacked from behind.

With every feint, Wolf had been distracting Raven, tugging her here and there, confusing her, making her forget Dragon. With every feint, Dragon had been inching closer, and now it struck! It leapt from a standing start, catching Raven by surprise, and its long jaws snapped shut round the end of one wing. Raven squawked in panic, pulled loose and lifted into the air, but Dragon flapped its stubby wings and chased after it.

That had been the gamble. Would Dragon attack or was it too soft and cowardly? But the old Construct had taken the chance. They would be evenly matched. Dragon was weak but Raven had been caught by surprise. It would be scrappy. Raven would win eventually – but meanwhile she wouldn't be thinking about Wolf…

Out of the darkness came Wolf's great looming shape, and the groundcrew grinned to each other. Lyall even cheered. Dolph pushed through the crowd and smacked him round the head, before scolding the rest to be quiet. Wolf settled on to her belly, cables dropped from above, and they got to work.

Coll, Fillan and the others unloaded the wagons, heaving the loops of anthryl and steel, tying them to the cables, watching as they were pulled up on to the deck. There was enough for months of normal use. Then the Tock equipment: endless grey boxes and electrical supplies. In the distance he heard the clash of metal as Raven and Dragon fought. It was too dark to see them, but lightning flashed across the plain and lit them up in frozen battle scenes.

"Is that it?" asked Dolph. Coll nodded and the big man grinned. "Good work, lads. Just the wagons to go."

The rain pelted around them as they dragged the wagons into position. Luna smiled at Coll, and even Lyall nodded. They had the equipment; Dragon would be dealt with, Raven weakened. It had worked!

"Coll, look," said Fillan. He pointed towards the sounds of battle.

Coll frowned and turned. "What?"

He heard a screech, but could make out only dark shapes in the storm, movement but no form. And then the lightning came again, once, twice, three times, lighting up the world in moments … and he saw.

In the first flash Raven was caught in Dragon's mouth, her whole body trapped. Her beak was open in a squawk, one wing flapping, the other hanging as if broken, her razor-sharp claws scraping against Dragon's steel face. Sparks flew.

Then the next flash – Dragon was swinging its head down hard, still holding Raven, and Raven was smashing down, her metal beak colliding with the ground, her neck snapping back with a crack like a thunderclap, loud enough for Coll to hear from where he stood.

And then the world lit up again, and Dragon was lifting its head, with Raven still in its jaws…

Raven was dead.

It hung limp, lights out, no movement at all. Small shapes fell from it – pieces of casing, or perhaps humans. Coll stared in wonder. As he watched, Dragon dropped the remains and gave a roar of savage triumph that echoed over the plain.

Then it turned, gazed at Wolf, and started running towards them.

"*Coll!*"

Coll shook his head. Fillan was pulling at his shirt, and he realised that Dolph and the others were rushing to Wolf's side. Wolf was clambering to her feet as Rudy bellowed orders.

"The wagons," Coll found himself saying. When did Dragon get so *strong*?

"Leave them!" roared Dolph. "Battle stations!"

Coll raced towards the cable and grabbed it. He tugged and felt it pulling him upwards. But as he looked down, he realised Fillan was still on the ground, staring at Dragon.

"Fillan!" he snapped. "Grab a rope!"

Fillan ran, but each cable seemed just out of reach. Coll cursed, lowered himself and dropped the last couple of metres, landing with a *thud*.

"You idiot!" he shouted. "Come *on!*"

Wolf was moving, with the last few groundcrew clinging to her side. Coll dragged Fillan into a run. "Come back!" he roared to Wolf. "Crew down! Crew down!"

He saw Rudy and Alpha shouting urgent orders on deck, but they didn't see him. He called again, "Crew down! Rudy! Crew down!"

But Dragon was close, and Wolf was getting ready to fight, paying no attention to them. Beside Coll, Fillan gasped as he tried to keep up. They were too late...

A single tether flicked down and landed in front of them, and Coll leapt and grabbed it with one hand. With his other, he held fast to Fillan's wrist. The cable whisked along the ground, dragging them.

"Coll!" shouted Fillan. "Help!"

"Hold the rope!" bellowed Coll. "Get a hold of the rope!" The ground scraped past them. Behind him, Fillan's weight seemed to suddenly drop, and Coll looked back in alarm, but then realised the boy had looped one hand round the cable. With relief Coll let go of him.

"Pull us up!" he yelled, but the rope didn't move. Groaning, Coll climbed. Rain lashed against him, and his world was nothing but flashes of Wolf's grey-white body. Glancing back, he saw Fillan still at the bottom, too weak to climb.

"Hold on!" he shouted. "I'll pull you up from the top!"

The boy nodded.

Coll heaved again and again. His arm felt strong and sure. He could do this. One metre. He could do this. Two metres. Dragon was almost on them. Wolf bared her teeth and shifted into a fighting stance. Three metres. Four—

"Argh!" Something wrapped itself round his head. Coll tried to drag himself free, but now there was a heavy shape too. He held on and looked up to see the Tock girl Rieka, in a thick black cloak, clinging to the rope and staring at him as if astonished. What was she *doing*? How was this helping?

"Don't climb down, you fool!" he roared. "Pull us *up*!"

"I'm sorry!" she said. Her face was pale. For some reason she was carrying a backpack.

"What?"

"I'm really sorry! I didn't know you were there!" Her hands were white with strain, and her feet were swinging free.

"Just pull us—"

She slipped, screamed and fell. Coll had just time to duck his head before she landed on his shoulders, knocking his right arm loose. All his weight, and hers, dragged against his prosthetic arm, and the hand slid down the rope with a sound like a shriek. Down they fell, colliding with Fillan and sending him flying – and then they smashed into the ground. Coll's head cracked against a boulder and the world suddenly filled with light and dark and a noise like ringing steel.

He growled, forced himself up and saw the rope whipping away. His fingers touched the end of it—

It was gone. Rieka was on top of him, he could hardly breathe, and his head felt like a spinning coin. He saw Wolf ready herself for Dragon's attack. He was close enough to feel Wolf's Call: *Wolf, Wolf, Wolf—*

Dragon smashed into Wolf and knocked her aside with one heave. Wolf yelped. Her teeth glinted silver in the darkness. Dragon lumbered forward again and snarled.

Wolf? thought Coll in confusion. What was happening? This wasn't the Dragon he remembered, the silly creature of weak wings and colours, laughed at and sent packing in the past. This Construct was larger, stronger, its body covered in heavy armour plating, even the deck hiding its crew. Coll could feel its presence, strange and furious and *so much more powerful* than Wolf's. Wolf leapt, but Dragon swung its tail in a vicious arc and smacked the other Construct down.

Wolf got shakily to her feet and jumped again. She tried to get her jaws round Dragon's throat, but its metal skin was impervious. It was unstoppable. It was *appalling*. When it roared, Coll's head rang. Wolf jabbed once, twice, again, but it was like fighting a mountain. She retreated once more – and now Coll saw Rudy on the bridge, staring down at him in horror…

Then Wolf turned and fled.

"No!" Coll croaked. His head ached like white fire. "No, come back!"

Dragon lifted its head up to the night sky and roared, and charged after Wolf, and Coll watched as they raced away across the plains and were gone.

8

FALLEN

When Coll awoke, the world was quiet.

He lay on his back, looking up at a strange green roof. Had they repainted the den? The roof rippled in a breeze and he realised he was in a tent. And suddenly he remembered everything that had happened – Raven, Dragon, the cache, falling, *everything*. He sat up in a rush and cried out, "WOLF!"

A red blot of pain shuddered through him, and for a moment he could hardly see. He ground his teeth until it passed and then felt at the back of his head. There was a large round lump. As he touched it, the pain shuddered again. He waited for it to fade and then crawled out of the tent.

It was early morning. The storm had cleared and the air was cold and fresh, the grass damp under his hands. A wood fire burned with white smoke, and piles of equipment lay around. Rieka was there, still in her thick cloak, with her backpack open beside her. She was standing next to a thin metal tripod and holding a device, studying it and frowning.

"Take it easy," she said without looking at him. "You hit your head."

Coll stared at her. He stood up, and staggered as a wave of dizziness threatened to blow him over. He looked to the south-west, where Wolf had fled.

"What happened?" he asked. His voice was croaky and his throat hurt. He was desperately thirsty.

"Dragon attacked," Rieka said, still not looking up. "Wolf ran. You fell and hit your head. Quiet now. I'm concentrating."

Coll blinked. Rustling came from one side and Fillan appeared, dragging a reel of rope. He smiled when he saw Coll. "You were sleeping!" he said.

Coll nodded. He felt terrible.

"I fetched all this!" said Fillan, swinging his arm around at the equipment.

"Shush!" hissed Rieka.

Coll turned back to her. "Are you looking for Wolf?"

"What?" she muttered, tapping the device. "No, of course not."

Coll's fists clenched. None of it made sense.

Wolf … *Dragon* … and Rieka on the cable…

"You did this!" he shouted. "You knocked us off! Stop whatever that is and *look at me*!"

Rieka sighed and stood up straight, facing Coll. "Yes," she said. "Sorry."

"*Sorry?* Why didn't you pull us up?" He waved at the stand. "What's all *this*?"

"It was an accident," said Rieka. "I didn't know you were on the rope."

"But you were climbing *down*!" he roared. "Couldn't you tell Wolf was moving? Did you *want* to be left behind?" Then he stopped. He looked at her cloak and the bag and frowned. "You were… I mean, you were…"

She shrugged. "I was leaving, yes."

"*Leaving?*"

"Yes."

"Leaving *Wolf*?"

Rieka rolled her eyes. "*Yes*, Coll. I was leaving Wolf."

Coll shook his head. Dark spots shimmered in front of him, and he felt dizzy again. *Leaving Wolf?*

"Are you all right?" asked Rieka. "I think you may have concussion. You should sit—"

"We're going," interrupted Coll. He turned towards the south-west. "We need to catch up with Wolf."

Rieka sighed. "She'll be twenty klicks away by now, maybe more."

"We're going *now*," snapped Coll. He walked off on trembling legs, trying not to let her see how weak he felt. "Fillan! We're leaving."

Fillan looked at him and then at Rieka. He dropped the equipment. "OK," he said simply, and followed Coll.

"Coll—" started Rieka.

Coll ignored her.

It was hot. The cool morning air burned off, and the sun hung heavy and angry over them. Coll and Fillan walked, saying nothing. The young boy seemed happy to follow him, skipping to keep up, gazing at the landscape and whistling under his breath. Coll gritted his teeth and concentrated on each step, trying to ignore the pain in his head. He was still thirsty, and they had no water. No food either. Twenty kilometres was a long way. He carried on.

What was Rieka *doing*? Leaving Wolf? Abandoning her crew, her home, her *life*? Leaving Wolf and stranding Coll and Fillan at the same time! Sorry, she said! Like it was nothing, leaving them here *on the ground*, like, like *Worms*! Up over a small hill and down the other side he trudged, his feet as heavy as clay. What was she *thinking*?

"Coll?" asked Fillan.

"What?"

"Are you OK? You were talking."

Coll stared at him. "No I wasn't."

Fillan frowned. "Oh. OK."

Up the next hill and down, scrambling through thorn bushes. And the next, and the next. This one seemed incredibly steep, and Coll felt the urge to crawl up on all fours. His head was full of thunderclouds, thick and black and pressing against the inside of his skull. But at the same time he felt strangely light…

He tottered to the top and stopped in surprise. Wolf was there! The huge Construct was standing only a kilometre away. Her mouth was open, her tongue lolling in a smile.

"Wolf!" he gasped.

"What?" asked Fillan.

Coll turned to him and grinned. "Look, up ahead! Come on!" He pushed his aching legs into a trot. "Wolf!" he shouted. "Wolf, wait!"

He was close enough to see the deck and even some of the crew. Rudy was there, waving to him, and Luna, and the enormous figure of Dolph. And there was Alpha, smiling and beckoning…

"Wolf, I'm coming!" he called. "Alpha!"

But as he watched, Wolf turned away and he realised she was leaving. "No!" he croaked. "No, Wolf, wait!

Alpha! Wait for me, Alpha! It's me, Coll! Wait!"

"Coll?" called Fillan, behind him, but Coll ignored him.

Wolf was running now. Weirdly the crew were still smiling and waving to him, but Wolf was leaving...

"No!" he cried. "No, please! Alpha, *please!*"

He stumbled on, his lungs burning. Black spots darted in front of his eyes like flies and he waved his hand to shoo them off, and then stared at his mechanical fingers. They seemed fascinating...

He bent over and was suddenly very sick. He staggered on two more steps, and then the ground swam towards him, and then he was *on* the ground, looking up at the sky, and then there was Fillan's round face gazing down.

"Coll?" Fillan was asking, but his voice seemed far away. "Coll?"

Coll tried to speak, but his tongue wouldn't move. It was as if it was too big for his mouth, like Wolf's. That was it! He had a long Wolf's tongue! He laughed, and Fillan's face disappeared. Coll felt his tongue, still laughing. He wondered if he was going to be sick again. The sky was very blue. And then there was someone else there and he smiled.

"Alpha," he murmured. "You came back for me."

Alpha leaned in. Her face curled into a scowl.

"*Idiot*," she snarled.

Coll's heart sank. "Oh, it's you, Rieka. Where's Alpha?"

Rieka sighed and turned away. "Help me with him," she said to someone. Then Coll was being dragged. The blue sky became dark, and then black, and then there was nothing.

"How are you feeling?"

Coll blinked. He was lying down inside a green tent. It seemed oddly familiar. Had he been here before? Rieka was sitting next to him.

"Th—" His throat clogged and he tried again. "Thirsty."

Rieka nodded and held out a cloth dripping with water. The drips landed in his mouth, and he swallowed with a feeling of incredible relief. His whole body wanted to absorb the water like a sponge. Rieka let him drink a little more, then stopped.

"Enough for now," she said. "Back to sleep, OK?"

He tried to nod, but something told him that moving his head would be a terrible idea. He answered or thought he did. His eyes closed and he fell asleep.

He wasn't sure how long this went on for – waking up to find Rieka or occasionally Fillan, taking little sips of water, falling asleep. Then soup, a mouthful at a time.

Sometimes it was light, sometimes dark.

And then one day he woke up and felt … better. He looked around. Fillan lay next to him asleep. Carefully Coll sat up. His muscles creaked, but he wasn't dizzy. He crept out of the tent and found Rieka still working at the strange metal tripod. Her device was fixed on top, turning slowly.

Rieka turned. "Careful," she said in a warning tone, and Coll nodded. It didn't hurt to nod. He reached to the back of his head. It was sore, but not the sickening feeling of before.

He crawled over to the fire and sat gazing at the flames. Rieka handed him a bottle of water and he drank. They sat in silence.

"Thank you," he said at last.

Rieka sighed. "I'm sorry for knocking you off the rope. I didn't mean to."

Coll still felt groggy, as if thinking was hard. From here he could see the remains of the battle. Raven lay on the other side of the plain, twisted and broken. That was important, and there was something about it – he should be worrying about something… And the cache – had Dragon come back to claim it? If not, why not?

But all he could do was remember Rieka's shocked face on the rope.

"You left Wolf," he said. "Did I remember that?"

Rieka bit her lip. "Yes."

Coll shook his head. "Why?" he managed. It made no sense.

Rieka started to answer, then stopped. Her face moved as if she was trying to find the words. "You know the device Intrick has for talking to people a long way away?"

Coll remembered Intrick had used it to talk to Wolf when they were at the cache. He nodded. Rieka pointed to the tripod. "This is like that but for listening. I built it when we were still on Wolf. And I picked up a … a signal, like a message. I don't understand it, but it's powerful. It's hundreds of klicks away, somewhere in the north. Whatever it is, I need to find it."

"Why?"

Rieka shrugged. "Because I'm looking for something that makes *sense*."

The sun was gentle on Coll's face. He wondered how long he had been sick. He felt oddly hollow. He remembered being furious, but it seemed a lot of effort.

"Wolf will come back when she's beaten Dragon," he said.

Rieka chewed her lip. "Maybe." Coll remembered the way Dragon had crashed into Wolf. When did it get so *strong*?

"I have to get back to her," he said. "You have to help me." He looked up. "Maybe there's something in the cache?"

"The cache is locked again," said Rieka. "I don't have the tech to access it."

Again, Coll wondered why Dragon hadn't come back for the cache. Surely that had been its target? But nothing about the Construct made sense. It had defeated Raven. It had *destroyed* Raven. It was after Wolf…

Coll scrubbed his face. "Rieka, I *have* to get back to Wolf. She needs me. I *have* to. *Please.*"

Rieka sighed and put down her scanner. She seemed to think for a long time, and then nodded.

"I need to go north," she said. "You want to go after Wolf. We both need transport. If you help me, I'll go with you until you catch up with Wolf. OK?"

He blinked at her. "Really?"

"You have to do what I say, OK?"

Coll frowned but he had no choice. "OK. But where's this transport?"

Rieka pointed across the plains. "There."

Coll stared. "Wait," he said slowly. "You don't mean…"

Rieka gave a thin smile. "Yes," she said. "I mean Raven."

9

BROKEN BiRD

Coll stared across the plains at the ruined Construct. "We can't use Raven," he said. "Raven's *dead*."

"It's just a machine," said Rieka. "I can fix it."

Coll wasn't sure about that. Constructs weren't just machines. *Wolf* wasn't just a machine. She was alive in a way he couldn't quite explain. She lived through her crew.

Her crew…

"Oh no," he gasped. Raven's crew! In horror he realised he hadn't even thought about them, but they must still be there! How long had he been unconscious? How long had they been camped here with their fire burning, visible to the enemy? He spun and faced Rieka. "Their *crew*, Rieka!"

"It's OK—" she said, but Coll grabbed her arm.

"It's not, they'll be coming for us! They'll have

seen us—"

"Coll—"

"Come on!"

"Let me go, idiot!" Rieka dragged herself free and folded her arms. "The crew's gone."

Coll stopped. "What? What do you mean?"

"I mean, gone," she said. "Not there. Gone. I saw some people on the first night, but by the morning they'd left. All there's been since is a few Ants scavenging for parts."

Coll frowned. "But … that makes no sense. If Raven could be repaired, her crew would never leave. It would be like leaving Wolf!" He glanced at Rieka and blushed. "I mean … you know."

Rieka nodded. "Maybe, but there's no one there now. So what do you want to do? It's this or wait for Wolf to return."

Coll thought. Wolf *would* return, wouldn't she? They wouldn't leave crew behind. But … perhaps they knew Rieka had chosen to leave. Fillan had just arrived, was hardly Wolf at all. And as for Coll… Surely Alpha would come back for him, wouldn't she? Wouldn't she? Coll rubbed his arm. Yes, she would. If she could. But they'd have to defeat Dragon. They'd have to *survive* Dragon.

Wait or go to Raven. Raven the enemy. Raven whose crew was gone…

He chewed his lip. "All right," he said at last. "We'll take a look."

Rieka insisted Coll take another night to recover, and after the last time Coll didn't argue. Instead, they spent the day getting packed and ready. Rieka collapsed her equipment and when Fillan woke up (delighted and excited to see Coll up and about), he took Coll foraging for supplies. Fillan was surprisingly good at foraging. He seemed to have an instinct for finding berries or fruit, or leafy plants they could eat.

"Radishes," he said, pulling one out of the ground. "They taste of pepper. And this kind of leaf with the crinkly edge. And these berries, I *love* these. One time I ate a whole bush full, and then I was sick, and it was *purple* sick!" He laughed. "But they're OK to eat a few."

Coll followed him around. "What about these?" he said, plucking a few tiny red berries off a bush.

Fillan shook his head. "Bad," he said. "Bad, bad, bad. They made me poo." He screwed his face up. "*Very* bad."

Coll spat them out. "You're pretty good at this," he said, and Fillan beamed. "Where did you learn?"

"I just did. After…" Fillan stopped. "I just did," he said. He wandered on ahead, pulling up roots and plucking fruit. Coll realised he still wore the little leather bag round his neck.

Fillan turned back. "Come on, lazybones!" he shouted.

When Coll caught up, the little boy took his hand and Coll let him.

They set off early the next day. It was a warm morning, and the long yellow grass was already dry. It rustled as they walked, and *swished* as the wind rippled through it.

They saw Ant tracks and occasionally Coll thought he heard their "chick-chick" questions. He still had his zapper with him and he kept it ready, but they saw nothing. They came across scattered pieces of metal and plastic, and Fillan discovered a long black steel feather almost as tall as him.

Then they found half a wing that had been torn away by Dragon's terrifying jaws. Metal struts poked out like bones, electrical cables dangled and hydraulic fluid had stained the ground.

"We're close," murmured Rieka.

The grass was flattened in patches around them. It felt like a battlefield, but everything was eerily silent. Just the swish of the grass, the tramp-tramp of their own footsteps and the buzz of insects. And a feeling at the back of Coll's neck that they were being watched.

They came to the edge of a crater, and there in the

middle were the remains of Raven.

She lay where Dragon had smashed her down: sprawled out, her metal feathers shoved out of place, one wing trapped underneath, the other gone. The razor-sharp beak was snapped in two. Her neck was twisted back horribly.

Coll thought about what Rieka had said. *It's just a machine*. But it wasn't.

Boxes and canisters lay around. Some might have been flung clear in the crash, but others looked like they'd been unpacked afterwards. There were Ant tracks, but also human footprints.

"Where did they go?" Fillan murmured.

Coll gripped the zapper, but Rieka ignored them and studied her scanner.

"No internal power," she muttered. "The central core has shut down." She turned to Coll. "I'm going aboard."

They clambered up the side of the missing wing. Rieka climbed awkwardly – Tocks weren't used to this kind of thing – but Coll found handholds among the feathers and heaved himself up to the top first and peered over the deck rail.

Nothing. It looked a little like Wolf's deck. There were seats with harnesses but no one in the seats. The deck had twisted in the crash and broken metal struts pushed out at odd angles. Something about it seemed … soft, as if its edges were blurry. As if it was melting in some weird way.

"Coll!" hissed Rieka behind him.

"It's OK," he said. "There's no one here." He leapt over the rail and almost stumbled. He realised he'd expected it to be moving, but it wasn't, of course. It was dead. Rieka followed, then Fillan. The wind curled through the deck with an eerie whistling sound. Somewhere a door banged.

"It's reverting," said Rieka. She saw Coll's blank expression and pointed to the soft edges. "The anthryl is holding everything together as Raven, based on the crew's psychic field. But the field is collapsing and the anthryl is reverting." She seemed to think this was an explanation. Coll had no idea what she meant.

"Right," she said briskly. "I'll check the processor; you find food."

Coll bristled. "What, are you Alpha now, giving orders?"

She gazed at him. "You get food," she said, as if talking to a small child, "while I access the central processor, recalibrate the sensors, analyse the damage report and initialise for cold start. I mean, unless *you* know how to do that?"

Coll glowered. "Fine."

She made her way carefully along the ruptured deck to

an entrance and disappeared.

Coll turned to Fillan. "You heard her," he growled. "Hop to it."

Some of the boxes on the ground had rations and supplies – water, dried meat, flour, grains, even medical supplies. Coll and Fillan gathered enough to keep them going for weeks.

"They must have brought these out after the crash," said Coll. "Why not take it with them?" The door was banging still, somewhere inside. Was it the wind? Coll frowned. "Stay here," he said.

Fillan looked at him, and then around at the silent site. He swallowed. "OK."

Coll went back up to the deck and climbed down through the entrance. A shadow moved behind him and he realised it was Fillan.

"Stay," he said again.

"OK," said Fillan.

Coll took another step and the boy followed.

"Fillan, *stay*," he snapped.

Fillan looked back towards the deck. Then, without speaking, he stepped closer and grabbed Coll's hand.

Coll sighed. "Fine. But keep back. I don't want to trip over you."

Together, they crept down the steps and into the belly of Raven.

It smelled different to Wolf – different people, different food – and the hairs on Coll's neck rose. Different was bad. The layout was strange too. The corridors were wider but lower, and painted dark, with flickers of green like leaves. Glimmers of light came from occasional portholes.

The banging came from up ahead, a closed door at the end of the corridor. Coll crept forward and carefully rested his palm against it. *Thump. Thump.* Whatever it was, it was on the other side of the door. Coll took a step back and then jerked as another face appeared in the gloom. "Argh!"

It was Rieka. "I heard it too," she whispered.

Coll held his zapper tight. "Fillan," he muttered, "go back to the end of the corridor." He nodded to Rieka. "Ready?"

"Do you think we should?" she asked. For once she seemed unsure.

Coll's heart pounded but he nodded. Carefully he reached for the handle. He waited for the next *thump* and timed his action.

Thump… Thump…

He turned the handle and wrenched the door open,

and a small blue blur hurtled out past him, crashed into the opposite wall and stopped, shaking its head.

It looked up at Coll. "Chick-chick?"

It was an Ant. "Chick-chick?" it said again. Then it seemed to notice Rieka and scuttered backwards. "Chick-chick!" Coll pointed the zapper but the Ant didn't react. It was quite a small one, just half a metre long. There was a dent on its head and it looked unsteady.

"Chick-chick!" it shouted. It raced up the twisted corridor towards Fillan but slipped, staggered sideways and shook its head. It tried to run on the floor, apparently not realising the floor was at an angle. It tried again and again, and then tipped on to its back.

"Chick-chick!" it wailed, waving its legs in the air. "Chick!" Then it stopped and its legs sagged. "Chick-chick-chick," it muttered sadly.

Fillan laughed. "That made me JUMP!" he said. "Funny Ant!"

Coll blew out a long careful breath and relaxed. He'd been holding the zapper so hard it was digging into his skin.

Rieka glanced inside the room. "Supply cupboard," she said. "It must have been scavenging and the door closed."

"Poor Ant," said Fillan. "It's stuck. We should help it."

Rieka shook her head. "No. If it returns to its nest, it might lead the others back. Leave it here and keep the corridor door shut."

Coll peered out of a porthole. "It's getting dark," he said. "We should eat."

They returned to the ground and Coll lit a fire and cooked up soup.

"I've made progress with the servers," said Rieka. "I think we can do something."

"There's plenty of supplies at least," said Coll. "It's strange, though. They brought all these boxes out..."

"Why didn't they take them with them?" asked Rieka, nodding. "It's the same in the server room; they haven't shut anything down. Wolf Tocks would *never* leave their station like that."

The sky was clear above them. It would be a chilly night, but no one suggested sleeping on board. The wind was picking up and the grass swished.

"What was that?" asked Coll suddenly.

"What?" asked Rieka.

Coll frowned and stood, staring into the darkness. "I thought I heard something," he muttered. "Maybe the Ants coming back. Hang on."

He took a step out into the dark. Was there something? A movement? He lifted his zapper. Another step...

"CAW!"

Col caught a glimpse of metal flickering past and he jerked to the side, swinging his prosthetic arm up in defence. Something clashed against it and he felt warning signals ripple against his stump like sparks.

"CAW!" screamed a voice again, and something leapt at Coll's head. He staggered and tripped.

"What the—"

"CAW!" A feathered shape loomed over him, dark and fierce, kicking and scratching at his face. Coll tried to defend himself but the shape was everywhere, a terror of whirling limbs striking again and again. Finally he managed to grab one wrist and then the other.

"Stop!" he shouted.

But the creature lowered its head and pecked at him with a hard stabbing lunge, its jaws snapping centimetres from his throat.

"CAW!"

Coll felt his arms weakening. The thing dived for his throat again.

"CAW!"

10

BRANN

The creature lunged at Coll's head and its jaws closed with a *snap*, missing his nose by a millimetre. It pulled free of his hold and swung a claw at him again.

"CAW!"

Coll raised his left arm and again there was a metallic *clash*. But this time Coll fell back, letting the attacker tip forward on to him. He raised his legs and heaved, throwing it away, and it smacked against a tree. He scrambled to his feet again and finally he got a clear look at the creature.

It was a girl.

She looked somewhere between his and Fillan's age and was wearing a feathered cloak. Slicks of lank hair half covered her face, and her mouth was drawn into a snarl. A wide black stripe was painted across her face at eye level, and her eyes glared out dark and fierce. Her 'claws' were blades in each hand. She was thin and quite pale.

"CAW!" she screamed again, racing forward and sweeping with her blades.

Coll grabbed a long branch and swung hard. The branch cracked against her feet and she collapsed with a yelp.

"Stay down!" he shouted.

Rieka and Fillan ran forward. "What's going on?" asked Rieka.

"It's a *Raven*," said Coll. "This is a trap! It's an ambush!" He stared up at the trees around them. How many more? How many hiding in the grass, getting ready to attack? He stood over the girl and raised his stick. "Where are they?" he demanded.

"Coll," said Rieka, "she's not—"

"Tell me!" he shouted.

The girl scrabbled away and stood up painfully. She held up her knives in defiance. "CAW!"

"Stop that!" Coll snarled.

"*Coll*," insisted Rieka, "*look* at her."

Coll frowned, but looked again and saw what Rieka meant. The girl was very thin, he realised, and filthy. The look in her eyes was hatred … or perhaps desperation? As he watched, she glanced from side to side as if trying to work out where to run.

"Are you Raven?" asked Rieka.

The girl glared at her. "You're *Wolf*," she growled, and spat on the ground.

Coll's hackles rose and he lifted the stick again.

"Coll, *stop!*" said Rieka. She turned back to the girl. "Yes, Wolf. But we're not here to harm you."

The girl's panting slowed, and her arms lowered a little. "Go away," she muttered.

"Or what?" sneered Coll. "You'll peck me? Peck-peck-peck, little bird?"

Rieka rolled her eyes. "Don't be stupid. Can't you see what's happened?" Coll glowered at her, but Rieka ignored him. "Raven is gone," she said to the girl in an unusually gentle voice. "Your crew have left, haven't they?"

The girl said nothing. Coll saw her pulse beating in her neck. She was trying not to show it, but she was terrified. He realised he was taller than her, and bigger, and he still had his stick. But she still had her knives...

Rieka, in that odd soft voice, said, "Do you know where they went?"

The girl didn't react at first, but then gave a tiny shrug.

"I'm Rieka," said Rieka. "This is Fillan, and Coll.

We're not a threat. Look, Coll's going to put down his stick, see?"

Coll blinked. "What?"

"Shut up and do it," hissed Rieka out of the side of her mouth.

Coll clenched his jaw, but threw the stick down. It clattered in front of the Raven girl and she flinched.

"See?" said Rieka. "Not a threat. I'm Rieka, this is Coll, that's Fillan behind us. What about you – what's your name?"

The girl stared at the stick as if expecting it to turn into a snake, but eventually she whispered, "Brann." She lowered her knives just a little.

Rieka beamed. Coll wasn't sure he'd ever seen her smile before. "Hello, Brann," she said. "Can we sit here?" The girl nodded, and Rieka sat. "Thank you. We'll all sit, OK?" Fillan sat down. Rieka tugged hard on Coll's leggings. "*Sit*," she hissed, and he half sat, half collapsed beside her. Rieka smiled again. "See? Now you, Brann. Will you sit with us?"

Coll scowled and leaned into Rieka. "She is *Raven*," he muttered. "What are you doing?"

"She's like us," said Rieka calmly, not looking away from the girl. "She's stranded, on her own. I think she's been on her own for days. Am I right?"

Another nod. Rieka smiled. Her smile really disturbed Coll. It was quite a *nice* smile; it was just weird seeing it anywhere near Rieka's face. "We've got soup, Brann. Would you like some?"

The girl stared at the soup pot for a moment, then back. She swallowed, and Rieka nodded encouragingly. "Fillan, could you fetch some soup for our guest?"

Fillan brought a bowl and Rieka offered it. "There."

The girl hesitated, and then put down one of her knives and took the bowl. She sniffed at it, then took a sip. Then she made a sound that was like a sob, dropped her other knife and grasped the bowl in both hands. She ate it without a spoon, drinking in huge gulps, gasping in between.

Coll glanced at the knives. Could he get to them while she was distracted? But Rieka put her hand on his arm.

"It's OK," she said, half to him and half to the girl. "It's OK."

The girl took a last gulp, tipping the bowl up to catch the drips. She started to breathe normally, and then gave Rieka another small nod.

Rieka smiled again. "What happened here, Brann?" she asked. "Where are your crew?"

The girl's face deepened into a scowl.

"*Dragon*," she snarled.

She spoke in short sentences, as if unused to hearing her own voice. She hadn't eaten in three days, she said. And the weeks before had been frantic, desperate. Raven's territory was far north of here, beyond the the Salt Cliffs, but Dragon had attacked them.

"We knew Dragon," she muttered. "Dragon is *weak*. Dragon is *foolish*. But…"

But this Dragon had defeated them, and Raven had been forced to flee. Down past the settlements of Fastvale and Beak, down through Sorrow Forest, with Dragon constantly at her feathers.

"It wouldn't *stop*," she hissed. She looked angry, but there was fear in her voice. "There's something wrong with it. It's not like us. We gave way, but it kept attacking; it wouldn't stop! Again and again, until it forced us out of our own land, down into Hyena's. We thought if we could get Hyena between us and Dragon… But Hyena ran too. And then we were in Wolf's realm, and *still* it followed us! We were tired, and we needed repairs…" She glared at Coll. "Then the *dog* attacked us."

"You were in our territory!" he snapped.

Rieka coughed. "Tell us what happened next," she said softly.

In the flicker of flames the girl's face seemed to shift:

the black paint around her eyes, the white of her skin, the trails of dark hair, her gleaming eyes. She became half bird. "We needed supplies. We saw some of the dog scouts, and we watched when they found the Cache. But Dragon came *again*. We were so tired. We were…" She blinked. "Dragon destroyed us," she whispered.

Nobody spoke. Coll found himself imagining what it would be like to see Wolf broken like that. Of course Wolf *wouldn't* get broken. Wolf wasn't Raven. But…

"Afterwards, we did what we could," she said. "Claw said we could survive and rebuild—"

"Claw?"

Brann frowned. "Claw. Our leader."

"You mean Alpha," said Coll.

"I mean CLAW!" shouted the girl.

Rieka lifted a hand. "Sorry," she murmured. "Wolf is different. Go on."

The girl glowered. "*Claw* said we could rebuild. They sent us chicks to scout out, on the first night. But I went too far, and – and – and when I…" She stopped. "When I got back … they were … gone."

"What do you mean 'gone'?" demanded Coll.

"I mean they weren't there!" she shouted.

Coll sighed. "She doesn't *know*," he said scornfully. "All that and she doesn't even *know*. Or she's lying."

"I'm not lying!" The girl raised her fists as if getting ready to attack again.

"No, of course you're not," said Rieka, giving Coll a warning look.

Coll stood up. "*Fine*," he snapped. "She's not lying. She and her stupid bird brought Dragon here, she's the reason we're *in* this mess, and she knows *nothing*. Is that it?"

"It was Dragon," muttered Brann. "Dragon *took* them."

Rieka frowned "It can't have been. Dragon went after Wolf."

Brann set her jaw. "Dragon," she insisted.

Coll sighed. "It's late," he said. "We should get some rest." He stared out into the darkness, then at Rieka. "We should keep watch. You and me take turns."

Rieka nodded, and Coll was relieved. This Raven girl… For all her kind words, Rieka didn't quite trust her either.

The night was quiet. The Raven girl moved to the edge of the circle, just enough to feel the warmth of the fire, and sat with her cloak wrapped tight round her, glaring at Coll. But after a while her eyes drifted closed and she slept. Or pretended to – Coll couldn't tell. Coll settled down. His stumps were tired and aching, but he kept his prosthetics on, ready to move, and he slept lightly.

She was still there in the morning. Coll realised he'd been hoping she would flutter away, or whatever birds did. But when he awoke and looked around, she was glaring at him again. He grunted, got up and made porridge. Fillan added some sweet berries he'd foraged. He was delighted to have found them, and showed them to Coll, and then to Rieka, and then, after a small hesitation, to the girl. She looked at him blankly.

"It's OK," he said in a helpful voice. "They're not the poopy ones."

She frowned in confusion but ate the porridge.

Coll examined Raven's remains as they ate. It had been bothering him from the moment he saw it − the neck snapped backwards, the half-missing wing. The feeling of decay.

"Raven's dead," he said to Rieka. "I know you said it's a machine and it can be fixed, but … you can't fix this. A Construct needs its crew. It needs the *Call*. Raven is *dead*."

"It's not!" shouted Brann. "You're just saying that because you're Wolf!"

But Rieka said, "Brann, I'm sorry. He's right. We can't fix this."

"We just need to find my crew," insisted Brann. "Then we can fix her."

"But where?" asked Coll. "Something took them,

so you say—"

"It's true! Dragon took them!"

He shrugged. "Fine. Then where? *Where* did it take them?" Brann scowled but didn't answer. "Dragon's south now, a hundred klicks away for all we know. And the only way to catch it is in *this* –" he waved his arm at the wreckage – "and this will never fly again. Raven is *dead*."

He turned to Rieka. "So what's your plan?"

Rieka stood and searched the ground. She picked up a feather and scraped away the plastic and burnished metal until she was left with a tiny scoop of anthryl. She held it in her palm, silver grey and shimmering with that strange grainy texture.

"We have everything we need," she said. "Raw materials, working computers, anthryl … and the four of us." She looked at Coll. "You're right, we can't repair this.

"We're going to make a *new* one."

11

THE CONSTRUCT

"You know what this is," said Rieka, holding the little dribble of anthryl in her palm. "You know all the Constructs need it. But what exactly *is* it?"

She tipped her hand and it moved in its strange not-quite-liquid way. The tiny grey grains seemed to climb over each other like insects – half alive, half mechanical. "Anthryl isn't magic; it's technology. These are auto-assembling nanothread loops. They're like tiny smart machines and they bind Constructs together. And give them their shape…"

She nodded to Fillan. "Hold out your hand." She tipped the anthryl into his palm and pointed her device at it, tapping the screen. "Now, think of something you like. Something you *really* like. Try to see it in your mind. OK?"

Fillan nodded. He closed his eyes and, after a second,

the anthryl grains began to move.

They pooled and swirled, and then climbed up over each other, making a shape, which became a head. It had shaggy thick hair, and heavy eyebrows, and its mouth was a scowl. It was a boy's face – Coll didn't recognise it, but it seemed familiar somehow. It was a bit like Alpha, he thought, only younger. And angrier.

Fillan opened his eyes and looked at it in delight, and then glanced at Coll. "Very good," said Rieka. The girl Brann burst out laughing.

"What?" asked Coll, confused.

Rieka tapped her scanner again and the grains collapsed. "This is what Constructs are," she said. "We think about our creature. We imagine it – we create a *psychic field* – and the anthryl turns it into reality. *We are Wolf.* That's what it means. *We* are Wolf.

"The software handles some of the basics, like the dorm rooms and power systems, hydraulics, stuff like that. But the rest – the whole 'Wolf' or 'Raven' thing? It could be anything."

"No!" protested Coll. "Wolf is *special*! She's not just parts. She's *alive*; we can *feel* her!"

"Raven isn't some machine!" snapped Brann.

Rieka shrugged. "This is science. Reality doesn't care what you believe. It doesn't care about your *feelings*. It just

104

is. The point is, we have anthryl, we have material, we have a processor and we have people. Raven is wrecked, but we can make something new."

"But if this is all we need, can't we repair Raven?" asked Brann.

Rieka shook her head. "Raven's too big. It took a whole crew to sustain it, and now look." She pointed to the remains. "We can't bring it back. But we can let it revert, and then make something small that the four of us can maintain." She looked at Brann. "If Dragon really did take your crew, this is the only way to catch them, understand?"

Brann's face was fixed into an obstinate scowl. But eventually she nodded.

"Just till we catch Dragon," she whispered.

"And find Wolf," said Coll.

Brann shrugged.

"I'll reset the field now," said Rieka. "Stand back."

Suddenly Fillan raced forward. "Wait!" he shouted. He leapt up on to the wing and then on board.

"Fillan, stop!" snapped Rieka, but the boy had disappeared.

He returned a minute later, holding a sack.

"Got him!" he called. "He's safe! I got him!"

The sack was wriggling. Rieka groaned. "Fillan … is

that the *Ant*?"

Fillan grinned. "Yeah! I saved him!" He held the sack up, grinning proudly.

"Nobody cares about an Ant, Fillan," said Coll. Fillan looked confused, and Coll waved him down. "OK, well done, you saved the Ant. Don't let it go! If it makes it back to its nest, we'll just end up with more."

Fillan clambered down. "I'm going to keep him," he said. "He's all bashed, but I'll take care of him. I'll give him a name! I'll call him … Kevin."

"Kevin?" asked Coll. "Not, I dunno … Anthony?"

Fillan gave him a blank look. "No, why?"

Rieka coughed. "Are we *quite* done?" she asked icily.

Fillan nodded, still holding the squirming bag, and Rieka tapped at her device. "There."

At first nothing happened. Then Brann gasped. "It's gone!"

Coll felt it too. That slight sensation in the back of his head since they approached Raven – the aura of … *something* – faded away. As he watched, the feathers writhed and fell. The anthryl pulled away from them and they clattered to the ground, breaking into metal and plastic pieces. The wing sagged and ripped loose from the body, and the head shrank, leaving only the metal struts of its beak.

"No," whimpered Brann. Tears ran down her face.

Then came a rumble from inside and the deck gave way with a huge crash, falling into the carcass. Dust rose in a cloud, then settled. There wasn't much after that. The anthryl moved to one side with a strange shiver, like sand shifting, and Raven's remains lay like the stripped bones of a dead animal: plastic and steel struts, hexagonal panels, cables and electronics.

Raven was truly gone.

Brann sobbed.

Rieka ignored her. "Right," she said, rubbing her hands. "Now for the interesting bit."

"Remember, you have to think *alike*," Rieka said. "It only works if you all think the same. So I'll do the Tock stuff, and you lot do the, you know, *believing* thing."

"Right," said Coll. "So … do we all just think about Wolf, then?"

"Wait, I thought we were making Raven!" said Brann.

"Don't be stupid," said Coll, exasperated. "Of course we're making Wolf!"

Brann folded her arms. "*Raven*."

Coll glared at her. This stupid bird girl was just problem after problem! Why couldn't she just do what she was *told*? He rubbed his face and for a moment remembered Alpha doing the same. Was this what it was like to be Alpha?

He took a deep breath. "Look, we've got three Wolf crew here, so we've a better chance of making a Wolf than a Raven, right?"

"Raven is faster," said Brann. "Raven can *fly*."

"We don't know if this will even work," said Coll. "Or if we can keep it working. Do you want to find out while we're in mid-air?"

Brann scowled but didn't reply.

"OK," said Coll. "So, we all know Wolf. Brann, you've at least seen her. We just have to remember." He turned to Rieka. "Now what?"

"I'll activate the system in Construct mode," Rieka muttered, tapping her screen. "It's pretty straightforward – we apply our psychic template to the field input, and it will self-actuate and deploy."

The others gaped at her. She sighed. "Me start Construct. You think Wolf. Construct make Wolf."

"You don't have to be rude," said Coll.

"I'm only rude to idiots."

"That's—"

"OK, *go*," she said, and pressed a button. The anthryl pile suddenly spread out, tendrils stretching and pooling around the metal and plastic pieces, picking each one up before laying it down again. Perhaps it was working out what it had to use. It seemed alive.

Then Coll felt it, that sense in his mind of… of *something*. Like a sound, no, a song … Yes, a song they were all singing. It was like being back on Wolf again, that feeling of sharing, being together. He could feel, or hear, or see, the others in his mind, joined together in a song. A song they could change…

"Now," he murmured, and together they created a new song. A song of Wolf.

I am Wolf, he thought, closing his eyes. *I am the hunter of the high plains, the shadow of evening, the ghost in the night. I am strong, and fast, my claws are powerful, and death is in my jaws! My eyes are sharp, my senses keen. My thick pelt keeps me warm, my padding feet can run a thousand kilometres. Wolf. Wolf. I am WOLF.*

"Hmm," said Rieka.

Coll opened his eyes and gasped. The creature before him was…

Awful.

It was small, hardly five metres tall, with short bowed legs and a fat hunched body, covered in a weird mix of wolf fur, raven feathers and long boar bristles. Its mouth was stuffed full of more teeth than could fit, forcing it open; its eyes were red and insane; and long slavers of drool hung from its mouth.

"What happened?" he asked in horror.

Rieka shrugged. "I told you, its form comes from what you imagine."

"I never imagined that!" snapped Coll. He stopped and listened to the songs in his mind and groaned.

On Wolf, everyone sang together, *believed* together. You learned it as a tiny child and you never lost it, and there were always hundreds around you believing the same, keeping the song pure. Here there were only the four of them, and all their songs were different. Coll's Wolf was right – pure and noble, fierce and proud, perfect. Rieka's was similar, though faint – she was concentrating on the Tock stuff and only half helping. Fillan was trying his best, but he kept slipping into Boar. His 'Wolf' was round-bellied, with more bristles than fur, the teeth more like tusks…

And Brann's Wolf was horrible. A vicious, rabid dog, a slavering monster, a cruel and mindless creature, pure evil. Her Wolf was a barking, yelping force of death.

"Brann, what are you *doing*?" gasped Coll.

"What?" Brann asked. "That's Wolf."

"No it's not!"

Brann seemed genuinely confused. "Yes it is. That's what Wolf *is*."

Coll drew a long breath. He resisted the urge to rub his

face again. "That's… OK, maybe that's what it seemed like when you were fighting her. *But that's not Wolf.*" She stared at him. "Here, look at mine," he said. She closed her eyes to listen to the song, and then opened them again immediately.

"*That?*" she snorted. "*That's* what you think Wolf is? *The shadow of evening?* Hahaha!"

Coll clamped his lips together. "That," he said carefully, "is what you need to think. And if you don't, then we will never leave here, and we will never catch Dragon, and you will never see your crew *ever again.*"

She stopped laughing. When she spoke again, her voice was subdued.

"OK," she muttered.

Coll felt bad. That had been cruel, hadn't it? He coughed and shook his head. "OK, well, we'll try again," he said gruffly. "Fillan, good work – but remember: *Wolf* not *Boar.*"

"Yes, Coll."

Coll nodded to Rieka. She tapped the device and the horrible creature dissolved back to the ground.

"Go," she muttered.

I am Wolf, thought Coll. *I am the hunter of the high plains, the shadow of evening* – he cursed as he remembered Brann's laughter – *the ghost in the night. I am strong, and fast…*

And this time he felt the others singing the same words now, even the same tune… It was like sharing strength, being with a group who all believed the same thing, all thought the same thing, acted with one mind…

"Not bad," said Rieka.

Coll opened his eyes and saw Wolf.

It was still tiny, and its fur was still bristly and dark – the burnished black metal of Raven's wings now woven into a pelt. But the eyes were blue, and the gaze was intelligent, its teeth razor sharp. It was almost Wolf.

"That's it locked," muttered Rieka. "So long as we stay in the field for most of the time, and keep mentally topping it up, it'll stay in place."

"So now what?" asked Coll.

Rieka smiled. "Let's go and see."

The new Construct kneeled down, and Coll and the others clambered on to its tiny deck.

"I configured it smaller," explained Rieka. "So we can maintain it with just the four of us. One room inside, a bit of storage space. We'll sleep on deck." She looked around. "What do you want to call it?"

"Wolf," said Coll.

Rieka shook her head. "No, a different name."

"Kevin," said Fillan.

Rieka rolled her eyes.

Brann was holding the deck rail. It occurred to Coll that all the parts of this new Construct must have been Raven before. How much of this was familiar to her?

"Cub," she said at last. "It's a small Wolf. So Cub."

"Cub," said Rieka. "Hmm."

"Cub!" said Fillan.

Coll nodded. "OK. Cub."

"It's been a long day," said Rieka. "Let's get something to eat and start out tomorrow."

Later, they lay on Cub's deck and looked up at the clear night sky.

"You know," said Coll, "this might actually work." He turned to Rieka. "Thank you."

She shrugged.

Coll hesitated. "The other day, you said you were looking for something that made sense. What did you mean?"

Rieka didn't answer for a while, but at last she sighed. "The Constructs aren't right, Coll. Anthryl is technology. Unbelievable, incredible technology. But we use it to make big animals and then fight *other* big animals. We've got zappers and computer servers and bows and arrows. How did we get like this? Why do we fight all the time?"

Coll didn't understand what she meant. Constructs fought and that was it. But she seemed serious.

"I hate it," she said. "The fighting, the hurting... Technology is just a tool, you don't have to *believe* in it! It's not supposed to be like this. That signal I picked up – I don't know what it is, or what it means, but whoever is sending it is far more powerful than us. Maybe they know something we don't.

"So I'll help you get back to Wolf, if she's still—" She coughed. "I'll help you get back to Wolf. But then I'm going to find that signal."

She gazed up at the stars, her face set and determined.

"And perhaps I'll find a better way to live."

12

HELP

They started packing the next morning: the food they'd salvaged from Raven, tools, a couple of zappers, blankets, as much as Cub could carry.

It wasn't much. Cub was small compared to Wolf, only the size of one of the houses in Scatter. And there was something different about him today, Coll thought. Had his legs shrunk overnight? His head become larger compared to his body? His tail was definitely stubbier, and his body rounder…

Fillan staggered past him, heaving a canister of water, his short legs tottering as he moved, and suddenly Coll realised. This morning Cub looked younger. Not a small Wolf – a Wolf *cub*.

"Of course," said Rieka, when he asked. "It's nominative determinism."

"Um," said Coll.

Rieka looked at him as if, yet again, he had managed to surprise her with his stupidity. "We call it 'Cub'," she said. "In our heads the word 'cub' means 'baby wolf'. So overnight it's absorbed that idea and adapted. You give something a name, that's what it starts to become in your head."

"But that's no good!" protested Coll. "We can't be going around in an *actual* wolf cub; how will we fight?" He shook his head. "'Cub' is a stupid name, we need something like, like 'Beast' – or 'Killer'!"

Rieka sighed. "It doesn't matter, Coll. It's too small to fight anyway. It's just a way to get to Wolf. Now give me a hand with these crates."

"It *does* matter," grumbled Coll, heaving more stuff on board. "We're *Wolf*."

When everything was stowed, they climbed up to the little deck on Cub's back and strapped themselves in.

"What happens now?" asked Brann.

"We join the Call again," said Rieka. "And then we just … walk. The Construct will handle things, just like on Wolf."

"OK," said Coll, trying to sound confident. "Ready?"

They nodded, and Coll closed his eyes. He listened to the deck below him, just like on Wolf. There it was – that tiny vibration, the shared song. He let himself sink into it and felt it around him: the beating silver blood of the Construct…

I am Wolf.

Cub stood on short shaky legs. Pistons hummed and hydraulics whined as he turned his head, and power came in little bursts as his crew tried to stay in harmony.

I am Wolf. Wolf. Or … *Cub?* Am I *Cub?*

"Wolf!" shouted Coll to the others. "Not 'Cub', 'Wolf'! Remember!"

"But he's called '*Cub*'," said Fillan, looking confused.

"He should be *Raven*," hissed Brann, and suddenly Coll felt the Construct remember wings and the tips of feathers and the perfect whisper of air currents lifting him up… "WOLF!" he roared.

Brann grumbled, but the image of wings faded.

I am Wolf.

"All right," said Coll. "We're going to walk now, nice and easy. Ready … go."

Cub pushed forward with his back legs, spread his front legs wide and tipped straight down on to his face.

"Argh!" shouted Rieka.

Fillan squealed and grabbed his straps.

Cub heaved himself back to his feet and shook his head. Coll tried to figure out what had happened.

"OK," he said, keeping his voice calm. "We'll try that again, but this time let's all remember that wolves have *four* legs."

"It's not *my* fault!" said Brann. "Four is a stupid number of legs! It's so complicated! I don't even know which goes first!"

"It's *obvious*!" snapped Coll. He pointed to the legs in turn. "Left-back left-front right-back right-front, one-two-three-four, *everyone* knows that!"

Fillan nodded and Brann's face turned red.

"Not *everyone*," said Rieka. Her voice was soft but she was glaring at Coll.

Coll clenched his fists. "All right," he said after a few seconds. "No. If you'd spent your life on a … a *bird*, you might not know that. Let's try again."

They tried again. *Walk*, thought Coll. It wasn't like Wolf at all. On Wolf everyone just *knew* what to do without even thinking. Now they were having to learn again.

Walk…

Cub took a half-step forward, and then another, and another. Its gyroscopes whined and Coll felt the Construct's delight and fear as the ground kept coming. He could hear Brann muttering "one-two-three-four, one-two-three-four" behind him.

"We're doing it!" he shouted. "We're walking!" He

looked ahead. "Hang on, this is the wrong direction. We need to turn round."

"Yeah?" muttered Brann. "One-two-three-four, how do we do that then? One-two-three-four—"

"Just stop for now," said Coll.

"One-two-three-four, *how*? One-two-three-four—"

"STOP!" shouted Coll.

Cub lifted his front paws, held them out like wings, and smacked head first into the ground again.

"Oof!"

"OW!"

"Brann!"

"It's not my *fault*!"

There was a silence.

"All right," said Coll at last. "Good. That was good. Let's … try again, OK?"

Slowly Cub tottered south. Grassland was easy enough, flat and steady. After a while, they got the hang of turning, although Brann had to shout out the legs over and over to stop herself from accidentally attempting to fly. They tried running, but it ended badly.

"I can't count that fast!" complained Brann.

"You don't have to count," retorted Coll. "You just *run*."

"I'd like to see *you* 'just flying'."

In the end, they settled for a peculiar half-trot. It was faster than a human could walk, but not enough to catch up with Wolf.

"That's not the real problem anyway," said Rieka, and Coll nodded glumly. The real problem was they had no idea where to go.

At first, the grass had been churned up by Wolf's paw prints and Dragon's massive gouging claw marks. But then they reached the river and a bed of loose scree on either side. After that there was bogland. There was no trail.

They stopped for the night on the brow of a small hill, and Fillan led them on a foraging tour. He ordered them all about in a high bossy voice, clearly enjoying knowing things the others didn't. But later he made stew, and Coll admitted it was delicious.

Rieka stayed back, working on Cub's systems. After dinner, she brought something out, and Fillan's face lit up.

"Kevin!" he shouted in delight.

The little Ant clattered forward and peered at Fillan. "Chick-chick?" it asked. "Chick-chick?"

"You fixed him!"

"Kind of," said Rieka. "Its signal unit was ruined, and

I had to reset the hive programming. It thinks you're its queen."

Fillan gaped at her, and then laughed. "Thank you!" He patted the Ant's head. "Who's a good Ant? You are! You're Kevin the Ant, yes you are!"

Kevin did a strange little shuffle, almost like a dance, and Fillan laughed again.

"Great," said Brann. "The annoying puppy has an annoying puppy." But she didn't say it unkindly. Fillan laughed again.

Later, Rieka and Coll stood and stared out at the countryside.

"Nothing," said Rieka, peering through her binoculars. "No trail. They've could have gone east or west. Maybe even south into the Glass Lands."

Coll considered. The Glass Lands were deadly. The earth there was black and charred, or glimmering as if half melted, and there was no clean water or food. Would Alpha have risked taking Wolf there? A few tiny pinpricks of light glimmered to the west and Coll pointed.

"That's Scatter," he said. "The settlement. Maybe they can help? They might have seen her…"

Rieka frowned. "Scatter's a Wolf town. They may not like another Construct sniffing around."

"The mayor knows me," said Coll. "He knows I'm

Alpha's… He knows I'm with Alpha."

Rieka lowered her binoculars and studied Coll. "Why do you find it hard to say?" she asked. "That she's your mother?"

Coll ducked his head. "I don't," he said, embarrassed. "I mean, it's just that she's Alpha first, that's all. That's more important."

Rieka frowned again. "Is it?"

Coll didn't answer. The last light went and a cold breeze came through the air. He shivered and rubbed his arm. "Anyway, what other plan is there? Let's go to Scatter and see what they can tell us."

Rieka shrugged. "All right."

By the next day Cub was walking better, even trotting along quite happily. Brann was still counting legs under her breath but less often. Once or twice they even managed a little half-run for a few steps, bouncing as the suspension adapted to them. Soon they could make out Scatter's buildings sprawled on the side of the hill. The sharpened posts of its stockade wall gleamed pale in the morning sunlight.

"They've seen us," said Rieka, pointing. As Coll looked up, figures appeared along the walls, and the front gates pulled half closed.

He nodded. "What do we do?"

Rieka shrugged. "Don't know. All go in?"

Coll looked back at the others. Fillan was staring at the town with wide eyes, his face pale. It hadn't occurred to Coll before, but this must be the last place he would ever want to see again.

"I'll go," he said. "Mayor Ruprecht knows me."

Rieka gazed at him. "Sure?"

"Sure." Coll tried to seem confident. "We're just looking for directions, right?"

They were close now, just a hundred metres away. There were no flags and banners this time. Cub pulled to a halt and managed not to fall over, and Coll climbed down.

As he walked towards the gate, he passed the sign again.

SCATTER

UNDER WOLF

He was aware of the people watching from the walls, holding crossbows ready. He tried to remember how Alpha walked – that confident, arrogant stride that showed she wasn't afraid of anything. He kept as straight and tall as he could and pretended he didn't notice the weapons.

Mayor Ruprecht was waiting, still in his dusty top hat and long coat. As Coll neared, the mayor held up a metal

123

loudhailer and bellowed, "That's close enough!"

Coll stopped.

"This is a Wolf town!" shouted Ruprecht. "We are under Wolf's protection! You have no right to be here!"

"Mayor, it's me!" called Coll. "Coll, remember? I was here before with Alpha. I'm Wolf!"

The mayor lowered his loudhailer and peered at Coll. He stepped forward. *"Coll?"* He glanced at Cub uncertainly, but then turned to the others. "Weapons down! This is Alpha's boy! Open the gate!" He shook his head. "Coll, my lad, what in the moon is going on?"

"…but now we've lost her trail," said Coll, later.

He and the mayor sat in the parlour where they had met before. Ruprecht had summoned up more of the little teacups, and now he gazed into his cup with an expression of worry.

"And Dragon," he said. "It's really become so powerful?"

"It destroyed Raven," said Coll. He coughed. "Alpha will figure out a way, though."

The mayor looked serious. "We'll do everything we can to help, of course. Excuse me." He stepped outside, and Coll heard him talking urgently to someone. When he returned, he was nodding. "I've sent a signal to recall our

124

scouts. If Wolf has passed, they'll know."

He gazed out of the window. "And that … *Cub*, did you say? That was actually Raven, before?"

"Yes," said Coll. "Rieka is a Tock. She showed us how to use it."

"Extraordinary." Ruprecht shook his head. "But vulnerable. You must beware – there are those who would do almost anything for wealth like that. Why, the anthryl alone…" He turned. "Do you need weapons? Do you have any way to protect yourselves?"

"I… Not really. Cub's based on Wolf, so he has claws, and teeth…" Coll thought about Cub's short stubby legs, the big, rather friendly face.

There was a knock at the door and a man entered. He wore a long brown leather jacket, dusty and out of place in the neat parlour, and he had a thick black moustache that drooped around his grim mouth. The man closed the door with a careful *click*, then muttered something in the mayor's ear. Ruprecht nodded.

"This is Samson," he said, gesturing to the man. "He tells me we've seen Wolf."

Coll felt a flood of relief. "Where?"

"Heading south," said Ruprecht, and frowned. "Towards the Glass Lands apparently, but we'll know the details soon. All we have to do is wait. More tea?"

Coll grinned. "Sure!" He looked at the man. "Anything about Dragon?"

Samson stared at him with no expression.

The mayor said, "Not yet." He turned and poured two more cups of tea and held one out. "Here you are."

As Coll took the cup, a little of the tea slopped out and the mayor scowled.

"Ach! Excuse me." He took a napkin and wiped the outside of the cup. But as he did so, Coll noticed something odd. Ruprecht was still smiling and chatting, but his hands were trembling. His forehead was faintly shiny with sweat. The man Samson stayed where he was, with his back to the door.

And suddenly – but, oh, too late, far too *late* – Coll realised that the faint *click* had been the lock turning.

"Now, then," said the mayor, holding out the cup. He smiled again, with a glint in his eye. "Drink your tea."

13

UNDER WOLF

Mayor Ruprecht offered the cup of tea to Coll and smiled.

"Here," he said. "While we wait."

Behind him, Samson, the man in the brown coat, said nothing. Coll looked at the cup rattling on its tiny saucer.

We are Wolf. He heard Alpha's voice. *If you admit weakness, your allies will turn on you, your enemies will strike.*

"Thank you," he said, and took it.

The door was blocked and locked. The windows were closed. Coll might be big for his age, but these were two grown men. He was trapped. He wondered whether Ruprecht had even recalled the scouts, but guessed he probably had. He'd want to make sure Wolf wasn't nearby. He'd want to make sure Cub really was weak. He'd even asked as much – *do you have any way to protect yourselves?* – and Coll had told him! Stupid!

The mayor watched him carefully. Coll lifted the cup

to his lips and pretended to take a sip. Was it drugged? It hardly even mattered. There was no way he could get through the door with Samson there. And what were the mayor's people doing now? Closing in on Cub perhaps. Fooling Rieka, like they'd fooled him? Luring them inside? Coll tried to imagine what Alpha would do. But Alpha wouldn't have walked in unprotected. Alpha wouldn't have shown *weakness*. And Alpha wasn't here. So: never mind what Alpha would do – what would *he* do?

Coll rubbed his knee. "Sorry," he said, putting the cup down. "My, ah, leg, you know? It gets stiff."

He stood slowly and limped round his chair, making a show of stretching. Mayor Ruprecht smiled wide and his teeth gleamed. "Quite all right, my boy," he said. "Make yourself comfortable, please."

"So your scouts saw Wolf, you think?" asked Coll casually.

"Certainly, certainly."

"But you don't know where."

The mayor said nothing. Behind him, Samson pulled his coat back a little and casually rested one hand on his knife.

"Sorry," said Coll again, shaking his head. "I'm a bit woozy suddenly."

The mayor's smile grew even wider. "Sit," he said

softly. "Take a rest."

"Yes," murmured Coll. "Yes…"

He tipped forward, resting his hands on the back of the chair. Then, in one movement, he swung as hard as he could and heaved the chair at the back window. The chair collided with the glass with a huge smash, opening a jagged hole and taking some of the window frame with it. Without even pausing, Coll charged towards the hole.

"Stop him!" shouted Ruprecht. Samson ran forward, but Coll reached the window first. Shards of glass pointed up like teeth. Coll leapt, covered his face with his arms, curled up into a ball—

—and was out.

Glass splinters flew about him as he tumbled to the ground. He rolled and scrambled to his feet, looking around wildly, and realised he was on the main street. Startled townsfolk stared at him. He turned and saw Samson clambering through the window frame and, behind him, Mayor Ruprecht, red-faced and furious.

"Get him!" shouted the mayor, pointing. "Get the boy!"

When Coll turned back, the crowd was hostile. It surged forward and Coll backed away, but the street was too full of people and he had no idea where to go. An old lady in a grey shawl looked astonished as he bumped into her. Then she whacked him hard with her walking cane.

"Ow!" he yelped. He shoved her away and bounced against the next person. It was the girl he'd seen before, the one who'd attacked Fillan. She'd looked mean then – now she was feral, reaching out for him with sharp bony fingers.

"He has a Construct!" shouted the mayor. "If we get him; we get *it*! Catch him!"

Coll pushed away from the main street and down into narrow lanes, driving himself on. He spun round a corner and another without thinking, trying to create a gap between him and the crowd.

"There he is!" shouted a voice, and someone appeared ahead of him, a large woman surrounded by tiny children. She was holding a rolling pin and blocking the way. Coll staggered to a halt, tripped, slid and crashed into her legs, and she stumbled and fell.

"C'mere, you rat!" she shouted, swinging the rolling pin. Coll lurched back to his feet and kept running. His breath whistled with every step and his lungs ached, and he could hear the mob behind him. Part of him was still screaming that this made no sense – Scatter was a Wolf town; it was loyal to Wolf! *He* was Wolf! But the baying, screeching roars told him all he needed to know.

Through a vegetable patch, over a fence, scrabbling up to the top of a wall and running along for five desperate steps, on to a flat roof, down into a garden, through a doorway into one of the houses, past an astonished-looking man holding an armful of laundry, leaping through the open window, and on, and on…

And suddenly he was at the stockade wall at the southern edge of the town. A set of steps climbed to a platform near the top, and Coll scrambled upwards, trying to ignore the sounds of pursuit and how close they were – they might grab him at any time. He could feel their breath on the back of his neck; he was too late, too *late*—

He reached the platform and peered over. On the other side was a drop of three metres, perhaps more. Coll swallowed and squeezed between the sharpened spikes. He hung for a moment, staring down at the drop…

"GOTCHA!"

A hand clamped down on his arm and Coll yelped and looked up. Samson was there, grinning with glee. He reached for Coll's other arm, but Coll swung away and hung from the man's grip. Desperately he tried to wriggle loose, but the man held tight. He tried punching Samson's arm with his free hand, but Samson hardly seemed to notice.

"Boss, I got him!" he shouted.

The man's fingers were like iron round the metal of Coll's left arm, and Coll's elbow twanged unpleasantly as the prosthetic sent strange twisting signals to his stump. He remembered the feeling. It had happened before, hadn't it?

He suddenly remembered Rieka saying, *There's a weak point*. Back on Wolf, after the fight with Raven. After his arm had malfunctioned. A weak point…

Coll swung again, twisting against the arm. How had he triggered it before? Like this? Higher?

"What're you doin'?" demanded Samson, but Coll ignored him and twisted again and again. "Stop that! Stop—"

Coll's arm spasmed.

A bright white-blue arc flared out, and Coll cried out in pain, and so did Samson, as the electrical feedback flowed through his hands.

"Aargh!" For a moment, the man's grip seemed even tighter, and then he recoiled and let go, and Coll tumbled away and down to the ground. He collided with the packed earth and groaned as his left leg took the force of the fall and his knee buckled.

He stared up. Samson was glaring at him in fury. More heads appeared, and now someone was clambering over.

Coll couldn't move, could hardly breathe.

"Get him!" shouted someone.

Coll tried to tell his body to respond, but it lay exhausted and battered, refusing.

"Get him!"

And then—

"Coll!"

Coll blinked. Who was that?

"*Move*, you idiot!"

"Rieka?"

Coll groaned, rolled over and stared. It was Cub! The Construct was running towards them – *running!* – and on board Rieka and Brann and Fillan were shouting.

"Coll, come on!"

Coll crawled down the hill. He heard a *thump* as someone landed behind him, and he pushed himself to his feet, took a tottering step towards Cub, yelped in pain and almost fell, but kept going. A cable flicked down.

"Take the cable!" shouted Rieka.

Coll took one more step and threw himself forward. His left arm was still dead, but he caught the cable with his right hand and held on tight. Something scrabbled at his ankle but couldn't grab hold, and now Cub was moving, dragging him through the thin scrubland and away. The cable pulled him up and arms reached under his shoulders, heaving him on board.

"Coll!" Fillan's face loomed up in front of him.

Coll was too winded to speak, but he held up a thumb and Fillan grinned. Something flickered past, like a bird, and hammered into the deck beside him. It was a crossbow bolt. And then another and another.

"Heads down!" he heard Rieka shout. "Get out of here!"

Coll pulled Fillan down and stared back at Scatter. The front gates were open and townsfolk were spilling out – some on foot, some on bikes. One or two even had electric bikes, with a rider at the front and a bowman behind. They chased after Cub, and Coll could hear them screaming in fury.

"Where?" shouted Brann.

Arrows flashed past. Coll and Rieka looked at each other.

"South!" shouted Coll. "Into the Glass Lands!"

Rieka stared at him as if he was mad, but he felt Cub responding to their Call, turning and running. The Construct ran with a weird broken step, like a wooden toy. There was more screaming from Scatter's soldiers, as they realised where Cub was going.

Up ahead, Coll could see the dirty yellow river that marked the end of Wolf's territory, and the start of the

Glass Lands, two or three kilometres away. The grass petered out as they approached and became straggly and sparse, with patches of pale brown between. Now he could see the water, murky and covered in scum. The riders on their electric bikes were catching up and bolts thudded into Cub's sides, but they were nearly there.

"Ready?" Coll shouted.

"No!" yelled Brann.

"Then *be* ready!" he roared.

Five steps away from the edge. Four, three, two, one—

"JUMP!"

Cub leapt, driving with his back legs and stretching forward, and for a moment they hung in the air before crashing down. Cub landed on the edge of the riverbank and the Construct scrabbled desperately, slipped, then found a grip and heaved them across with a shriek of hydraulics.

Coll risked a look behind. The Scatter townsfolk had stopped on the other side, glaring at them. He thought he could make out the mayor in his top hat. No one wanted to risk touching the poisonous water, and no one was brave enough to try to jump it. An arrow fluttered towards Coll but fell short.

Coll collapsed with a sigh. "We're safe," he said. "They won't try to follow us here."

"Yeah," muttered Rieka. She stared at the desolate, dead world ahead of them. "Because who'd be crazy enough to enter the Glass Lands?"

14

THE GLASS LANDS

The ground was dark, sandy brushland, streaked with black and only a few yellowing thorn bushes for vegetation. There was no water anywhere, and the air was sharp in the back of Coll's throat. Parts of the ground glimmered like glass. Metal spars stuck out like strange trees, scorched and rusted into tattered ribbons. Coll had never been here but he'd heard the stories.

These were the Glass Lands, where nothing lived.

"How's your arm?" asked Rieka.

Coll carefully opened and closed his left hand, and twisted his elbow. "Better. Thanks."

Rieka scowled. "*Don't* do that again. I warned you about a malfunction that could cause serious damage, and you *deliberately made it happen*. I can't keep repairing it, understand?"

Coll nodded. "Sorry."

"Hmph." Rieka shook her head. "What happened in Scatter?"

"Mayor Ruprecht tried to take me prisoner." Coll looked back at the town, now just a dot to the north. "He said he would help, but he just wanted to capture Cub."

"Well, *duh*," said Brann. She was only half listening, still counting under her breath, but she made a scornful face. "What did you expect from Worms?"

"I expected them to respect Wolf!" snapped Coll.

"Who could respect *that*?" Brann scoffed.

Rieka raised a hand. "*Enough*." She glared at them both. "You don't get it, do you? Those townsfolk – the ones you call 'Worms' – they *hate* us."

"No they don't!" said Coll. "They're always pleased to see Wolf!"

"*Raven* townships show *proper* respect," said Brann haughtily.

Rieka nodded. "They fear us, because we can destroy them. But fear isn't love. And now you've told them about Dragon, we can't go back to Scatter or any of the other towns. Because the truth is out – Wolf can be defeated."

Coll frowned but didn't answer. The people of Scatter *loved* Wolf. The disaster with the mayor would never have happened if Wolf had been there. Rieka was wrong – of course she was wrong – he just couldn't work out why exactly. Alpha would know; if only they could find Wolf...

As if hearing his thoughts, Rieka said, "So where do we go now?"

Coll considered. Nobody went through the Glass Lands if they could avoid it. Even desperate, Wolf wouldn't go any further than she had to.

"South-east," he said, trying to sound confident. "It's the shortest route out."

"Assuming she came this way at all," said Rieka. "Maybe we're not even close."

Coll nodded glumly. But it was the only plan they had.

They carried on a few more kilometres before dusk. Coll wanted to push on, but Rieka refused. "We can't travel in the dark," she said. "The ground's too rough – if we take a wrong step, we'll end up spiked."

Coll reluctantly agreed and they made camp. Brann and Fillan prepared dinner from rations. They seemed to be getting along. Fillan's friendliness was infectious, piercing even the Raven girl's hostility. She bossed him around, but her tone was soft.

They stayed on Cub's deck and ate quickly and quietly.

"We'll have to preserve food and water," said Coll. "Everything here is poisonous."

Rieka nodded. "We don't have much."

The wind hissed constantly, pushing the black sand around. The skies were cloudy and low, as if the world was closing in. Coll was exhausted after the events at Scatter. He knew they should set up a watch and keep guard in shifts, but before he even finished the thought, he fell asleep.

The next morning continued in the same way. Rieka's devices told them they were heading south-east, but the ground was featureless, just endless blackened sand, fractured glass, rusty metal spikes and tough, vicious thorn bushes. The skies stayed cloudy, but it never rained and the air was hot. It smelled of red rust and tasted raw.

The crew's clothes became clogged with sand. They were all thirsty, but Rieka kept them on strict water rations, and there was none spare to wash with. The metal parts of Cub became too hot to touch, and hissed angrily as he moved. Coll's prosthetics were affected too, the cooling systems whirring and whining in overdrive, and sending him fluttering, confused signals. Sand worked into the joints and rubbed against his stumps.

At the end of the third day they ate in silence. Even Fillan was quiet. He leaned against Brann with his head bobbing, half asleep. At his feet Kevin the Ant turned and turned as if trying to get comfortable, and its joints crackled with grit.

Rieka pointed to a taller spike of metal, quite close. "We could climb that," she said. "Take a look ahead."

Coll nodded. "I'll come with you."

They left Cub and walked out over the ruined land. This evening it stank of sulphur. They climbed up the metal tower and gazed out into the half-dark.

"Anything?" asked Coll.

Rieka lowered her binoculars and shook her head. "Coll—" she started.

"Just a bit further," said Coll. "I know what you're going to say, but I'm sure she's down here somewhere. We must be close."

"We're down to less than half our water," said Rieka gently. "We've gone too far already, Coll."

Coll said nothing. Rieka was right. But if they turned back now, they would never find Wolf. He felt it in his heart.

They climbed down and walked back to Cub without speaking, stepping over the patches of splintered, glimmering glass. Suddenly Rieka stopped and put out a warning hand. When Coll glanced up, she nodded forward, her face tight.

Coll looked ahead. There was Cub, where they'd left him, but Fillan and Brann weren't on board. Instead, they were standing on the ground.

In front of them stood two strangers.

It was a man and a woman. The man was dressed in a long leather coat, and at first Coll wondered in alarm if it was Samson, Mayor Ruprecht's thug. But no – this man was older, with white shaggy hair and beard, and his jacket was ancient and patched. His face was marked with long cheerful wrinkles, as if he laughed a lot. He was laughing now.

Beside him stood a tall woman wrapped in layers of brown shawl. Her hair was grey and tied up with a piece of rawhide, and she had a strong, hard chin. She was smiling, but her face was careful. It was as if smiling was something she was choosing to do for now.

Fillan was chattering away to them, showing them Kevin the Ant. Brann stood slightly back, her face unsure.

Coll and Rieka exchanged looks. Rieka's expression was as worried as Coll felt. What should they do? They had to get back to Cub. Could they do it without being seen?

But as he thought that, the woman lifted her head, turned and stared straight at them, though Coll was sure they'd made no noise.

Fillan followed her gaze and waved. "Coll, Rieka! Look! *People!*"

The man turned. Rieka cursed, and she and Coll stepped forward.

"Evening!" said the man. He had a soft voice, slightly lilting, with an accent Coll didn't recognise. "Well met. We saw your camp, and your fine Construct, and thought we should say hello. Hello!"

Rieka nodded politely. "Hello."

Coll said nothing. He fought the urge to hide his prosthetic hand behind his back, but the man didn't seem to pay it any attention. Instead, he smiled at Rieka.

"Your Construct's a beauty," he said, gesturing to Cub. "And Fillan here tells me you're the one who fixed his Ant!"

Rieka didn't answer. The man chuckled and turned to the woman. "Reckon this is a cautious one, Mrs B," he said.

The woman nodded. "Doesn't like surprise guests, Mr B," she said. Her voice was low and soft.

"Reckon not," he agreed. He clapped his hands. "Well then, let us introduce ourselves! I'm Dolen, and this here is my wonderful wife, Namir." He grinned. "We're the Beetles."

He stepped to one side, and Coll saw that behind them, half hidden in the dark, was the strangest Construct he'd ever seen.

It was a beetle. Its body was split into three parts – a flat head, a large rounded body and a smaller round section at the back. It had six legs, like Fillan's Ant, but the legs were much thicker and stronger. The body was black and hard, like a shell, and covered in thousands of tiny neat dents. It was about half the height of Cub and perhaps a little longer.

"We're not here to challenge your territory," said Rieka quickly. "Really, we're just passing through; we didn't mean—"

Dolen tipped his head back and laughed. "Territory? By the moon, girl, who would want to own the Glass Lands?" He shook his head. "We just came to say hello is all. Check you was all right, see if you needed help."

"Why are you here?" asked the woman, Namir.

Rieka and Coll didn't answer. "We're looking for Wolf!" said Fillan.

Rieka swore under her breath.

Namir frowned. "Wolf? The Construct? Why?"

Coll sighed, but there was no point in denying it now. "Two Constructs," he said. "Wolf, and one calling itself Dragon."

"Hmm," said Dolen. "You're a long way into the Glass Lands for that. This is a dangerous place…" He and Namir turned to each other. He seemed to be asking her something, and after a second she dipped her head slightly. Dolen beamed. "Reckon we can help," he said.

"You've seen them?" asked Rieka. Her voice was cautious. "Where?"

Again there was a long pause. "East," said Dolen at last. "But the going is hard, and slow. If you want to catch them, there's a better route. We're heading that way ourselves."

"We're fine on our own," said Coll.

But Namir shrugged. "The east route is *very* hard," she said. "You don't want to try it. And you'll need water. We can show you."

Coll bit his lip. Beside him, Rieka was tight-faced.

Dolen grinned. "It's late," he said cheerfully. "We need our shut-eye, don't we, Mrs B? We ain't as young as we used to be!"

"That we're not, Mr B," agreed Namir.

"So we'll say goodnight," said Dolen, "and you can decide in the morning. How's that?"

Coll nodded. "All right."

The Beetle crew clambered up the side of their Construct, to a little cockpit just behind the head.

Dolen waved. "Goodnight!" he called. "See you in the morning!"

He smiled again. His smile was infectious, and Coll

found himself smiling back. But as the Beetle turned, Dolen and Namir exchanged a glance. And it seemed to Coll that, just for a moment, their smiles faded and in their place was something else.

Something wary.

15

THE BEETLES

"Well, *I* like them," said Fillan.

They were on Cub, a little later. Beetle had settled a hundred metres away and its crew, Dolen and Namir, had made camp. Their small fire glowed faintly green in the strange air of the Glass Lands, and Coll could smell cooking.

"We can't trust them," said Brann. "Constructs aren't *nice* to each other. What are they doing out here? What do they *want*?"

"Anthryl probably," said Coll. "Maybe everything we have – there are no resources out here." He frowned. It felt weird to agree with Brann.

"Well, they're right about water," said Rieka. "We've barely enough to make it back out, and if we do, the townsfolk could be waiting for us. We need to find some."

"We could take *their* water," suggested Brann. "Why

not? Cub's bigger, we've got more crew."

That had been Coll's thought too. But something about the Beetles made him cautious. They were tougher than they made out, he was sure. They were hiding something.

"Well, *I* think they're nice," said Fillan stubbornly. "And Kevin likes them too, don't you, Kevin?" The Ant looked up at Fillan and rubbed its antennae.

"If you want to find Wolf, they might be our only chance," said Rieka. She yawned. "Look, it's late. Let's sleep on it, decide in the morning."

Coll nodded. "Yeah." He stared at the other Construct. "But we sleep on deck in shifts. Someone awake at all times."

The others groaned, but nobody argued.

The next morning, Dolen laid a battered map on the ground and pointed out their route with a scrap of metal.

"South first, to the Ribbon – here," he said. "That's a smooth patch; it's easier travel. Then east, till we reach the Steel River. It's a day and a half maybe."

"The Steel River?" said Coll. "I've never heard of it."

Namir said, "There'll be game near the river, a bit of vegetation – we can stock up on food and water. Then we'll send you on your way and you can find your Wolf."

148

A day and a half of travelling would use up almost all their remaining supplies. If there wasn't water at the end of it... Coll turned to Rieka and she gave a tiny nod.

"All right," Coll said. "We'll go with you."

Dolen grinned. "Glad to have you with us. Ain't that right, Mrs B?"

"Oh yes," said Namir.

She didn't smile.

They set off, and Coll was impressed by Beetle's pace. Dolen and Namir must be powering it just by themselves, but it scrambled over the rough ground without stopping, its six short legs sure and quick. Soon Cub started to drop behind. His paws could run endlessly over grass, but struggled on the loose sand, slippery glass and metal spikes. Beetle slowed to let them catch up, but still the pace was relentless.

"Got to reach the Steel River in time, see?" said Dolen, when they stopped for a very short rest.

"Why?" asked Rieka. "What's there?"

But he just grinned again. "You'll see."

They reached the area Dolen called the Ribbon. Here the sand was densely packed like a road, which was easier to walk along, and Cub was able to speed up. They weren't the first to go along this route; scraps of plastic and metal littered the sides. Beetle stopped and poked at some as they passed.

"Look at that, Mrs B!" called Dolen, holding up a torn canister. "Bit of work, that'll be good as new." He lifted a panel in Beetle's large body and threw the canister in, then beamed up at Coll. "Can't be too fussy out here, you see," he said. "You survive long enough in the Glass Lands, you get so's you'd bottle your own sweat!"

The clouds had lifted, but the sun that beat down was harsh, reflecting off the glass in thousands of piercing lights, and Coll's head ached. The Beetle crew put on wide-brimmed hats and Dolen shrugged off his jacket, but Namir kept her shawl on, its heavy layers covering her shoulders and arms. The afternoon went on forever. Fillan started to doze off, and Brann's endless *one-two-three-four* sank into a mumbled drone.

But at last Beetle slowed and pulled off the road by a small hill. The Construct settled into its shadow and lowered its flat black body to the ground.

"Phew!" said Dolen, stretching. "I reckon that road gets longer every time we takes it, Mrs B."

Namir chuckled. "That it does, Mr B, that it does."

Cub settled in beside them and flopped to the ground in exhaustion. Its pistons and hydraulics gave a sad slow whine as they cooled. But the Beetle crew didn't stop – Dolen heaved out a cooker and set it up, and then rummaged around inside Beetle's body, removing some packets wrapped in greasy paper. Namir brought out a machine covered in pipes and placed a bottle underneath it. After a few minutes, a thin trickle of water started to pour from the machine. Namir watched it carefully, guarding each drip, and snapped the machine off as soon as the bottle was full.

"Does that machine make water?" asked Fillan.

Namir shook her head. "Recycles it," she said. "That means it makes it out of old water."

"Oh." Fillan's forehead wrinkled. "Where do you get the old water?"

Dolen gave a sudden booming laugh. "Best not to ask *that*, young 'un," he said.

Brann leaned down and whispered something in Fillan's ear, and the boy blinked in astonishment. His expression flickered between disgust and fascination.

"Can't waste anything in the Glass Lands, see," said Dolen.

"Why live out here, then?" asked Rieka.

"It's just what we do," he said cheerfully. But for a moment he seemed to glance at Namir, and she glanced back.

Rieka frowned.

"Grub's up," said Dolen. He lifted two sticks from the

151

cooker, with some kind of roasted meat on each of them. "Glass rat. Bit tough, but good eating. Who's first?"

The food wasn't as bad as Coll had feared. While they ate, they turned the cooker down to a low warmth. Namir was quiet, but Dolen was good company, telling stories of wandering the Glass Lands and adventures aboard Beetle. In return, gradually, the Cub crew told their own stories. The Beetles listened carefully, Dolen making noises of surprise and awe. Namir gazed at the glowing flames.

"Your Alpha sounds impressive," she said softly.

"Oh, she is!" agreed Coll. "She's a brilliant leader."

"It must be difficult sometimes, her being your mother too."

"Well…" Coll hesitated. "Yeah, sometimes. She has to look after the whole crew, see?" Namir said nothing. "But she protects me." Coll felt a strange need to defend her. "And she keeps me strong. I mean, when I was born, like this…" He held up his prosthetic arm. "She fought for me. For the anthryl to make my arm, my leg. And she fought the crew. Crews aren't comfortable with people who are … different. Some of them didn't … didn't want…" He fell silent, frowning.

Dolen smiled. "She sounds very dedicated. You

must be proud."

"Yes." Coll felt as if there was something missing, but he couldn't quite work it out. "And she needs our help. She needs me to be Wolf."

"So you're going to find her and show her?" asked Namir.

Coll nodded. Namir looked at the others. "You have your own Construct now," she said mildly. "You could go where you liked. You don't *have* to be Wolf. You could pick your own crew."

Coll shook his head. "Wolf is home," he said stubbornly, before the others could speak. "I *am* Wolf."

It grew dark, and the Cub crew were sleepy. Fillan was already snoring, and Brann's head dropped suddenly. She snorted and looked up, and Dolen smiled.

"Time for bed, Mrs B," he said, standing. He nodded to the others. "Good travel today. Early start tomorrow – we'll be at the Steel River by midday. Goodnight!"

Namir stood too, in a single smooth movement, and gave them a curt nod. They headed off, Dolen waving, and climbed up into the Beetle Construct.

The Cub crew dragged themselves up to their deck. Coll wondered for a few minutes about trying to keep guard again – but as soon as his head touched his pillow, he fell fast asleep.

The next morning he awoke with a start and scrambled to his feet. Falling asleep! Falling asleep right next to another Construct, unprotected and vulnerable! What would Alpha say? He ran to the deck rail and peered out, to see Dolen packing up the cooking unit and whistling.

"Morning!" called Dolen, waving. "Another day in paradise, eh?"

Coll blinked at him in confusion. The clouds had sunk again and the world was grey and pale and dismal. He shook his head. Behind him, he heard the others moving.

"Morning, Mr B!" called Fillan, and the man grinned and waved. On board Beetle, Namir emerged from a hatch and nodded to them.

Dolen climbed up next to her. "We'd best get on," he called. "The Steel River won't wait, eh?" He laughed, Beetle clambered to its feet, and they set off again.

The travel was easier today. The Ribbon road was solid and smooth, and the morning air was still quite cool. Cub was getting better at walking – Brann was no longer counting under her breath – and the four of them had settled into a rhythm. For the first time since leaving Wolf, Coll felt the sense of being part of a whole thing. *We are Cub*, he found himself thinking at one point, but then angrily corrected himself. *Wolf*. We are *Wolf*.

Again, Beetle scurried ahead of them. Occasionally Dolen glanced up at the sky, judging the time.

"Reckon we're close, Mrs B," he said at last.

"Reckon so, Mr B," she replied.

Coll looked around. He couldn't see anything except a low hill ahead. But when they came round the hill, Dolen looked back at them, grinning.

"There!" he called. "The Steel River."

Coll and the others stared.

It looked like a huge cave carved into the hillside. It was six metres tall, six wide, a black circle too perfect to be natural. Out of it came a channel that led to the next hill, into another identical circle. The sides of the channel were metal, rusted but still strong, and almost completely smooth.

The channel was as dry as bones. A thin layer of white sand lay in the bottom, and several small white boulders attached to the sides in a seemingly random pattern. They were each about the size of Coll's head but flatter, as if squashed.

"What is it?" asked Coll.

Dolen grinned. "This is your river, boy!" He jumped down from Beetle's cockpit and began fetching things out of the back.

"I don't understand," said Brann. "Where's the water?"

"We're just in time," said Dolen. "Can you feel it, Mrs B?" He dragged a dozen buckets from the back, and then some netting and a long sharp spear.

"Can indeed, Mr B," said the woman. And now Coll realised he could feel something too. The ground beneath his feet seemed to be trembling.

"What's going on?" he asked, but the Beetle crew were too busy to answer. Coll looked back at Rieka. "Rieka, what's happening?"

"How would I know?" snapped Rieka. She hated not knowing things.

"The ground is moving," said Fillan. He reached out and tugged at Coll's shirt. "Coll, why's the ground moving? Coll?"

"Ready?" called Dolen.

"For what?" demanded Coll.

"Ready!" shouted Namir.

And now Coll heard it – a deep rumbling sound was coming from the mouth of the channel, from inside the hill. First quiet, then loud, so loud he could hardly think.

"I think we should move back—" he had time to say, before he couldn't even hear his own shouting voice, and something glinted at the back of the tunnel, a white frothing wall—

And the cave exploded.

16
THE STEEL RIVER

Coll scrambled away, falling and landing on his back with an *oof!* and staring as the silver white wall exploded out of the cave. It crashed along the channel, and he realised in astonishment that it was…

Water.

A huge wall of water, more than Coll had ever seen, was charging like a Construct at full speed towards them and then past them along the channel, spitting and frothing, into the mouth of the opposite cave. It was so loud the sound itself felt like a physical force, shoving him back. The air filled with white mist and the ground under his feet turned instantly dark, the sand like mud, the glass slick and green.

"Whoo-hoo!" shouted Dolen. He lifted his arms, facing into the spray of water, and Fillan did the same.

"Whoo!"

The channel became a river. It was dirty at first, but after a few seconds it ran clear and the pressure eased a little, and Dolen and Namir began refilling their canisters.

"You should do the same," said Dolen. "It runs for thirty minutes, so take your fill."

Rieka was already digging out containers and barrels from Cub's storage, and Coll ran to help. They quickly filled everything they had with clear, pure water. Dolen brought out armfuls of dirty clothes and started soaking them and beating them against the steel sides, and Namir took a brush and washed Beetle.

It was like new life after the horrible desert. Rieka let the water soak her, her eyes closed as she rubbed her face. Brann and Fillan flicked spray at each other, laughing, then scrubbed the grime from Kevin's joints. The Ant stretched its back in happiness and shook itself dry in a scatter of drops.

Coll became aware of how dirty he felt. Dust and sand clogged his hair and stuck to the sweat on his face and was ground between his teeth. He leaned over the channel and ducked his head into the river, scrubbing his face and hair and letting the current carry away all the desert filth. Pulling out, he hesitated, glanced around, and then unfastened his arm. He rested it on the side and ducked in again, holding on with one hand. The water felt wonderful against his stump, soft and cool. He wanted to jump in, but he couldn't swim and the current was too fast. But he opened his eyes under the surface and watched the muddy trail leave him and head downstream.

As he watched, he noticed that the odd stone lumps on the sides of the channel had been prised loose by the water and were now moving. One slowly tumbled towards him, somehow drifting against the current. It had an odd thin line down the middle, he noticed. It came nearer and the line grew thicker, and then the whole stone seemed to open up. Coll stared in astonishment as it bobbed forward, the opening lined with small sharp stones that looked like … well, like…

Teeth.

And suddenly Coll realised the stone wasn't drifting, it was swimming towards him, *fast*, and its mouth was glinting with diamond-sharp teeth, and as he jerked his head out of the water the jaws closed in front of him with a *SNAP!*

"Argh!" he spluttered, pulling back. His one hand slipped against the wet sides and he plunged back into the water, losing his grip. The current seized him and dragged him under. He yelled again, but water muffled his shout and filled his mouth and he choked. All he could hear was the pounding wash, and the world was white and churning, turning him upside down. In a tiny moment of clarity he stared ahead and saw the horrible stone creature, its jaws wide open, and more behind it. It lunged forward, and Coll flung his arm up—

A spear stabbed through the creature, driving it down and pinning it to the bottom. A wispy trail of blood seeped out, and the other boulders turned and made for it in a feeding frenzy. Something grabbed the back of Coll's shirt and heaved him upright. He stared up.

Namir stood waist-deep in the water like an iron statue, her legs braced and unmoving in the current. Her face was as sharp as a blade, glaring at the rock creatures, and the arm lifting Coll bulged with muscle. Another creature drifted close and she drove her spear down again and stabbed right through its shell.

"Ups-a-daisy!" came a cheerful voice. Now arms lifted Coll and hoisted him from the water, and he realised they were Dolen's. On the bank, Fillan, Rieka and Brann were staring at him in shock.

"Got him, Mrs B!" called Dolen.

Namir nodded. Carefully she waded back, holding her spear aloft and scanning the water. She heaved herself out of the channel with one arm and stood, gazing down at Coll. Her eyes were flat and careful.

"All right?" she asked.

Coll gaped at her. "Y-yes," he managed, and she nodded.

She reached down and picked up her shawl, pulling it over her T-shirt. But before she did, Coll saw her arms. They were covered in tattoos, a single pattern of fluid stripes that ran from wrist to shoulder. Each stripe was solid black, three or four centimetres wide, waving and curling round her.

Namir saw him watching but said nothing. She stalked away.

"Well now," said Dolen cheerily. "That was an adventure, eh?"

The water slowed after a while, as Dolen had said it would. The raging river became a stream, and then a trickle, and soon all that was left were puddles in the bottom of the channel. The creatures settled down like boulders again. Coll stared at them with loathing.

"Rockjaws," said Dolen. "Nasty little critters, but they stay in the water. Should have warned you – wasn't expecting you to take a dip!"

Rieka gazed into the cave. "How often does the water come?"

"Every thirty days," said Dolen. "Like clockwork. Runs

for thirty minutes, then stops." He glanced at Rieka. "You're thinking something makes it happen, right? Sharp girl like you is already trying to work it out." Rieka nodded and Dolen smiled. "Often wondered myself. It comes from the north-west, maybe north – it's curved, I reckon. Beyond that…" He shrugged. "You could go inside and see where it ends up, but I don't recommend it – not with these fellas around!" He laughed and swept one arm towards the rockjaws.

"North…" murmured Rieka, sharing a glance with Coll.

Dolen stowed his now full water canisters and barrels, then pulled out the stove and made dinner. Behind him, Namir emerged from the back of Beetle and started tinkering with the water filter. She ignored them at first. But after a few minutes she stopped, smiled grimly to herself and sat down next to Coll.

"How are you?" she asked.

Coll had dried himself off, and refastened his arm. He gazed at her. "You're Tiger," he said.

Brann stiffened and leaned back. Rieka's eyes flashed. The woman said nothing. Dolen stirred his soup without speaking. "Those tattoos are Tiger," continued Coll. "Aren't they?"

"We're Beetle," said Namir. "That's all."

162

"But you *were* Tiger, weren't you?" Coll insisted.

Namir sighed. "I thought I was," she said quietly. "In another life."

Coll swallowed. Wolf's territory was large. She fought Raven and Hyena, and occasionally Puma to the east. This new thing, Dragon, was somehow stronger than them. But Tiger... Tiger was legend. Tiger owned all the far eastern lands, from Endwall to Silverhead. Tiger, Lion, Eagle, Bear – they were *gods*.

Coll turned to Dolen. "What about you?"

Dolen laughed. "As if they'd take a fool like me! No, no. I was just a bodger, getting about, selling this and that. A Worm, as you like to call us. And then one day I met Mrs B..."

"And I realised I wasn't what I thought," said Namir. Her face still had that blade-like sharpness, but it softened as she watched Dolen. "We created Beetle and we made a life."

Rieka looked around at the desolate landscape. "Not much of a life."

"It's *our* life," said Namir sharply, and Rieka looked down. Namir sighed. She lifted her arm and let the shawl fall away, revealing her tattooed Tiger stripes, and gazed at them in the flickering glow of the heater. "Where else could we go, child? With these marks? Any Construct would kill an exiled Tiger. Any township would hand us over. Folk aren't keen on different. Things they don't understand … they get uncomfortable. Scared even. Isn't that right, Coll?"

Coll shrugged. Almost without thinking about it, he pulled his sleeve down over his hand, and Namir nodded. "Tell me," she said. "Why are you so keen to find Wolf?"

"They need our help," said Coll. "And … it's *Wolf*. I am Wolf! And Rieka, and Fillan! We are Wolf!"

She smiled. "How would you know, if you've never had a choice?"

"Soup's up," said Dolen.

For the rest of the evening Dolen kept up his chatter, talking about the river and the Glass Lands and Beetle. After dinner he brought out a guitar and played as Namir sang. She was a good singer, and the night filled with ancient songs.

"Who's next?" asked Dolen, when she had finished. "You got a song?"

Coll shook his head, and the others pulled back. Dolen laughed. "Come on, you must know *something*."

Brann said hesitantly, "I know a dance."

Coll and Rieka stared at her and she blushed. But Dolen beamed. "Well then, show us, lass!"

Brann stood and did a little shuffling dance, moving her feet in quick double-steps. She lifted her arms as she stepped, and dropped them and lifted them again. Her face grew tight with embarrassment and she stopped.

Coll stifled a laugh, but Fillan said, "It's a bird!" He smiled at Brann's scowl. "It's a bird dance!"

"It doesn't matter," muttered Brann. She went to sit down again, but Fillan stood up beside her.

"Show me!" he said. "Please?"

Brann stared at him as if trying to decide if he was mocking her. But she showed him and he copied her steps. Dolen picked out a tune to go along with it, a high rippling note that curled and strummed like the wind. Fillan and Brann danced.

After a few seconds, Rieka stood and joined them, trying to copy Brann's feet. She was *terrible*. She tripped over Fillan and stumbled back and forth. She was as graceful as a rock. But Fillan just laughed happily, and even Brann gave a rare, awkward smile.

"Come on, Coll!" said Fillan.

"It's a Raven dance!" scoffed Coll. "I'm not doing that!"

"But it's fun!" said Fillan. He looked at Coll hopefully, until at last Coll sighed.

"*Fine*," he muttered. "Show me, then."

Dolen played his guitar, Namir clapped a rhythm and the Cub crew danced.

"See?" laughed Fillan. "It's fun, isn't it?"

Brann smiled again. Rieka's face was a mask of ferocious concentration. Coll shook his head but grinned.

After the dance, Brann said, "Fillan, your turn – show us something Boar."

Fillan looked awkward. "I'm Wolf now," he said, glancing at Coll.

But Brann insisted. "You were Boar once, weren't you? Come on, give it a go!"

So Fillan showed them a Boar game, with mock wrestling and butting. He was quite ferocious, crashing into them, roaring, even knocking Coll over.

"Yield!" Coll shouted, laughing.

Fillan grinned, and Brann held up his hand in triumph.

Then Coll and Rieka led the others to the top of one of the small hills.

"Feel it in your bones," Coll instructed them. "Let it come out any way it wants. It's a living thing, let it sing." He opened his mouth, felt the warm air around him, and howled like Wolf across the broken land. Rieka joined him, and their call spread over the air. Fillan's voice was high and short, like a yip. Brann's was a long *caw*.

The empty night listened, as the Cub crew howled to the moon.

The next morning, the Beetles prepared to head back.

Dolen pointed east. "The road carries on that way for twenty klicks or so," he said. "We saw your Constructs heading that direction. But they weren't on the Ribbon, and we'll have made better time. I reckon you'll catch them in a day or so."

Rieka nodded. "Thank you."

"Good luck," said Dolen. Beside him, Namir checked the straps and fastenings.

Rieka, Brann and Fillan climbed aboard Cub.

"Coll?" said Namir suddenly.

Coll turned.

Namir didn't say anything at first. She looked away, unusually hesitant, her eyes scanning the landscape as if trying to find words written there.

Eventually she said, "You know … from the moment you're born, people around you will tell you who you are. *What* you are. Every day they'll tell you." She shrugged. "And sometimes they're right. But sometimes … they're not. Sometimes you're not what they expect. Maybe they'll tell you that you're Tiger, but then you realise you're actually Beetle. Or Cub. Or something no one has

167

ever seen before."

She smiled. "When that happens, Coll … *you* have to decide. I hope you find Wolf, and Alpha. But the only person who really knows what you are … is you."

Before Coll could respond, she turned and leapt up into Beetle's cockpit. "Good luck!" she called.

Dolen waved. Then Beetle flexed its six legs, turned in a complicated shuffle and scrambled away.

Coll watched them go.

"Ready?" called Rieka from Cub's deck.

He nodded. "Yeah." He grabbed a cable, hoisted himself aboard and took a seat. He grinned. "Let's go."

17
WOLF

The Glass Lands changed as Cub's crew headed east. Gradually the scrubland turned green, the glassy sand petered out, and a faint breeze came up, clear and cool. Metal spikes still reached up out of the ground, but taller now and often wrapped round bricks and the remains of buildings.

Cub moved quickly along the Ribbon. It wasn't like Wolf's running – Cub's stumpy legs made each stride more like a little half-jump, half-hop, and his head bobbed as if he was excited. The movement jostled the crew around, despite the gyroscopes and stabilisers trying to keep them steady, but they'd got used to it. In an odd way it had started to feel right.

They looked for traces of Wolf. How far had she gone? Was Dragon still chasing her? When they stopped for lunch on top of a low rise, Rieka searched the horizon with her binoculars.

"Something over there," she said at last, pointing. "I can't make it out. Buildings or something."

They carried on and reached the ruins of a settlement, with rows and rows of scattered bricks and metal. Coll felt there was something strangely familiar about the remains. The houses were gone, but the foundations were still there, neat squares and ancient roads. He suddenly imagined a family standing in front of them…

"These are like the ones in the picture," he said. "Remember the picture in the Cache? Are these the same houses? Did something … happen?"

"What could have done this?" asked Brann.

Coll shook his head. It was creepy and they didn't stop.

Beyond the destroyed settlement the land changed again. Thorn bushes gave way to straggly grass and flies flew up around their heads in great clouds. The Ribbon tapered out and the ground became broken and muddy with marshy areas. But in other parts the ground was dry and dusty, and there still hadn't been any rain.

"I think this water has come from the Steel River," said Rieka. "I think it's leaking out."

Now there were potholes and sudden swampy patches that hadn't had time to drain away. They had to pick their way through them and it was exhausting.

As evening fell, Coll sank his head. "They're out there," he said to Rieka, though he wondered if he was actually trying to convince himself. "They're out there."

Rieka's lips pursed but she said nothing.

The next day was the same until lunch. Then Fillan pointed and shouted. "Look! Something on the ground!"

Cub halted and Coll climbed down. The earth had been churned up: great gouges carved out of the dirt. The scars were still fresh. And there—

He picked up a piece of steel plating, with a ragged edge of anthryl. "This is Wolf's," he said.

Rieka inspected it and nodded. She looked around. "Any more?"

They retrieved a pile of pieces, some small, some large. There were one or two Coll didn't recognise – Dragon's, perhaps? But most of it was Wolf's. Reaching under a thorn bush, he found a long tooth.

"It was a fight," said Brann. "And your Wolf lost."

"She didn't lose!" snapped Coll. "Wolf doesn't lose! Do you see a dead Construct around here? Like *Raven*?"

Brann scowled and ducked her head.

Rieka frowned. "There *was* a fight," she said. "And Wolf took damage. But we're on the right track."

They climbed back up on to Cub's back and stared ahead. There were marks in the grass – perhaps a trail?

171

But the swampy ground hid the rest.

Coll looked at Rieka and she shrugged.

"Let's go," he said.

They set off. Brann was still angry at Coll's comments, and it affected Cub – his head was down, his footsteps stomped, he kicked at stones as he walked. They carried on that way for an hour before Brann suddenly said, "This is stupid. Scrambling along the ground like bugs; this is *stupid*!"

"We're not flying," said Coll.

"But we *could*," insisted Brann. "We could. I could show you!"

"No!" shouted everyone, even Fillan.

"*But look*," said Brann.

Cub had just reached the top of a hill and was heading down the other side. And as he did so … something happened.

Coll felt as if there were two versions of Cub in his mind. One was the half-wolf, half-puppy they were used to. But the other was … thinner and wider, his nose longer and sharper, almost like a beak, and there was something growing out of his sides, long wide flat panels that caught the wind and lifted Cub up, and now his front feet were partly off the ground and his steps were like long gliding jumps, and then…

"Argh!" cried Coll.

Cub glided through the air for five metres or more, lifted by a gust of wind, and for a horrible moment the world was far below them and they were flying!

"Brann, stop!" shouted Rieka.

Brann ignored them, her eyes tight shut, her mouth in an obstinate line.

"We're a *bird*!" said Fillan, staring around them, holding Kevin the Ant tight.

Coll clung to his seat in horror. "Stop!" he cried.

Cub lifted again and now he was twenty metres up or more. He curved in the air.

"See!" shouted Brann triumphantly. "We can be Raven! Raven! CAW, CAW, CAW!"

"Brann, you can't do this!" snapped Rieka. "You can't maintain this form all by yourself; it's not safe!"

But then Fillan pointed. "Look, there's something there!"

"I'll bring him round!" said Brann. "He's not quite like Raven yet, hang on. I've got him. I've— Oh, wait—"

Cub wheeled in the sky, but his shape wasn't right. The thin wings weren't enough to carry his weight and one wing suddenly twisted and they plummeted downwards.

Rieka and Coll screamed, as Fillan shouted, "Wheee!"

"Hang on!" said Brann. "Hang on, I can fix it. I can—"

Cub tumbled out of the air, twisting and half cawing, half yelping. He smacked against the side of a hill and slid down through bushes and small trees. Part of him tried to flap his wings, part tried to brace his paws and he morphed and changed before landing at the bottom with a *thud*. Coll, loose from his harness, was flung backwards, out past the weird half-wolf-half-bird tail, then *yoinked* back by his tether, colliding with Fillan.

Everyone screamed.

Then there was silence.

Coll dragged himself upright and staggered towards Brann, who was shaking her head groggily. He reached for her, but Rieka stepped in between them.

"Calm," she said in a warning voice.

Coll bared his teeth. "That stupid bird girl nearly killed us!"

Brann shouted, "I was doing fine! We were *flying*!"

"We are Wolf!" shouted Coll. "Understand? Not Raven, *Wolf*!"

"This *was* Raven!" shouted Brann. "It's *my* Construct, and she was *Raven*!"

"Tell her, Rieka!" shouted Coll.

"Tell *him*!" shouted Brann.

"Enough!" snapped Rieka. "I'm sick of being in the middle of this stupid fight. You're *both* idiots!"

174

Coll and Brann fell silent, both glaring at Rieka.

In the pause, Fillan said, "Please don't fight."

Coll glanced down. Fillan's face was pale. He was trying to smile, but he looked scared. Kevin was cowering behind him. Coll wanted to snarl that it was *Brann's* fault, but... He clenched his teeth together and said nothing.

Rieka spoke. "Brann, trying to change a Construct form mid-travel against the will of the others is as dumb as mud. Are you smarter than mud? *Are* you? And, Coll, try *speaking* to Brann instead of just bellowing orders. And I am not here to separate you like squabbling *puppies*, so sort yourselves out!"

Brann looked like she was about to shout something, but instead she subsided.

Coll turned away.

Rieka said, "Fillan was right – there *was* something. I saw it too. Two or three klicks east at the end of the valley. It was just a quick glimpse, but ... I think it was Wolf."

Coll spun back and stared at her. "Really?" She nodded and suddenly all his anger disappeared.

"Come on, then!" he shouted.

"*See?*" muttered Brann. But Rieka glared at her and she ducked her head again.

They set off, four paws firmly on the ground this time. Brann didn't try to change Cub's shape again and soon they were scrambling along in Cub's half-skipping run over the grass and swamp, avoiding cracks in the ground. They reached the valley and there, at the far end, was...

Wolf.

Coll stared at her and gulped. *Wolf.* He wanted to shout to them – Alpha! Rudy! Luna! But they were too far away. Cub sped up, racing towards the Construct. It was so much larger than Cub; he'd almost forgotten.

"Wolf," he murmured.

Beside him, Brann frowned. "What's wrong with it?"

Coll turned in surprise. "What?" But then he realised what she meant. Wolf was limping away quite slowly. She was thinner than he remembered and covered in patches of metal and cracked carbon fibre; it looked like she had been fixed in a hurry, on the move. The repairs had pushed the long hairs of her pelt up into straggly tufts. Her head was down and one ear had been ripped away. He couldn't see her crew at all, and instead her back was grey.

"They've sealed her," said Rieka, looking through her binoculars, and Coll nodded. They'd fastened metal plates above her deck to protect themselves. It would have left them almost blind, unable to see out. It was something a crew would only do in desperation.

"Where's Dragon?" asked Fillan. "Did they win?"

The Cub crew looked around but saw nothing. "Maybe," said Coll.

Brann snorted. "No way."

Cub scrambled towards Wolf. She seemed not to notice them until they were close. Then she gave a start, leapt backwards in a weak, tottering jump and yelped.

"Wolf!" shouted Coll. "Wolf! Alpha, we found you!"

Wolf's face was scarred. As well as her torn ear, one eye was white and cloudy and there were deep scratch marks around her jaw. She glared at them.

"Coll…" said Rieka. "Be careful."

But Coll unfastened his harness and ran to the front of Cub. "Hoy!" he shouted, waving his arms. "Wolf! It's us! It's me! Wolf! Alpha!"

Wolf took another step back and crouched. Her hide was badly torn. She seemed to shiver. Her teeth were bared.

"Coll!" shouted Rieka, but Coll ignored her.

"Wolf!" he called again.

"Coll, take your seat!"

Coll turned to Rieka in surprise. "What?"

He looked back just in time to see Wolf leap towards them, her mouth wide open in a snarl, front claws out, ready to kill.

18

LOST

Wolf launched herself at Cub. Her one good eye was red and furious, her teeth ready to crash down on them, her front paws stretching their razor-sharp claws.

"MOVE!" roared Brann, and Cub tottered backwards. Coll almost lost his balance. He scrambled back to his seat and tried to fasten his harness. What was happening? What was *happening*?

"No," he croaked, almost to himself. "We're Wolf. We're Wolf!"

"Concentrate!" snapped Rieka, and Coll looked up at her.

"But we're *Wolf*," he said almost in a wail.

"She doesn't know that!" shouted Rieka, and finally Coll understood. He felt Cub's panic and tried to help, steering the Construct away. But Wolf was rabid and furious, snarling with rage and leaping at them again.

Her jaws clamped round Cub's right hind leg and there was an eruption of splintered metal before Cub wrenched free.

Wolf went for them again. Cub slipped to the side, only a metre away. There was a torn gap in Wolf's armour at the shoulder, and just as they slipped past, Coll could see through to the bridge and Wolf's crew.

He saw Rudy shouting orders and Intrick the Tock working at a console, Luna and the others in their harnesses. And at the helm, on the head deck, was Alpha. Her arm was in a sling but she gave no sign of weakness. She appeared as controlled as ever, and her face was steel. She glared through the slit in the armour and Coll stared back, and for a moment she looked straight at him…

Nothing.

Her expression didn't change. There was no flicker of recognition. No softness.

There was nothing.

Cub crashed to the ground and scrambled away, reaching the top of the valley. Wolf chased after.

"We've got to get out of here!" shouted Rieka.

Coll felt like he was underwater. Nothing. She'd stared straight at him. She'd *seen* him. Nothing.

Rieka shouted, "Coll!"

He looked back at Rieka in a daze.

"We can fly!" shouted Brann.

"NO!" yelled everyone. But Brann closed her eyes and again Coll felt the sensation of wings sprouting from Cub's back...

"Enough!" snapped Rieka. She turned to Brann and slapped her.

Brann stared at her in shock, and Cub's body morphed again and the wings disappeared. Behind them, Wolf reared up mid-leap, startled at this strange new Construct that seemed to change its shape in the middle of a fight. But then her working eye filled with fury again. Cub wasn't fast enough, strong enough or fierce enough – he had no defences – and here came Wolf's slavering jaws for the kill...

A deep roar echoed across the valley, booming and savage. Wolf pulled back immediately and turned with a yelp. Cub turned too and stared.

Dragon was there.

It seemed even bigger than before. Perhaps it was more patched – perhaps Wolf had managed to inflict some damage during their fighting – but it seemed strong. The old green and gold paint was almost entirely worn away now to a mix of greys. As it stomped towards them, Wolf cowered, turned, and fled.

"Run away!" shouted Rieka. "We can't fight Dragon. Run away!"

Coll nodded and tried to focus, and Cub scrambled away in the opposite direction. Dragon passed them without stopping. Like Wolf, its deck was sealed with large metal plates, as it had been before, and he could see no crew – just the fierce, relentless, sharp-toothed mouth. It followed Wolf out of the valley. As it did, Cub tripped and tumbled down, shaking the crew inside, before finally coming to a standstill.

Coll slumped in his seat. His ears were ringing and his shoulders were agony where the harness straps had held him. He saw Alpha's face in his head over and over. She'd stared straight at him and not recognised him. All she'd seen was an enemy Construct. Nothing else. Not even Coll. Her … her *son*.

"Ow…" muttered Brann behind them.

Coll's jaw clenched. He unfastened his straps and turned on the girl. "You!" he spat. "You did this!"

Brann had a cut on her forehead and looked dazed.

Coll didn't care. "Treacherous Raven!" he hissed. "*Vicious* Raven, this is what you wanted all along!"

Beside her, Fillan looked up. "It's not Brann's fault," he said in a reasonable voice.

"Yes it is!" snapped Coll.

Rieka said, "Don't be an idiot—"

But Coll turned on her now. "Stop calling me that!" he roared. "You did this, too! You're the reason we're even *here*! On this stupid thing, this stupid … *Cub*! We are Wolf! *I* am Wolf! She didn't even *recognise* me!"

Rieka stared at him in confusion. "Who didn't?"

Coll spun back and stabbed a finger at Brann. "You made wings again! You never believed in Wolf! You're the reason she didn't recognise us!"

"Coll, Brann's one of us," said Fillan. "She wouldn't—"

Brann stood up and faced Coll. "It's not my fault your stupid Wolf can't see!"

"Yes it is!" he shouted. "She saw me! Alpha *saw* me!" He wasn't even sure what he was shouting about.

"Then your Alpha's as stupid as you!" snapped Brann.

Coll shoved her hard and she staggered back, tripped and fell to the deck.

"Coll!" shouted Fillan in alarm.

Coll ignored him. He stood over Brann with his hands clenched into furious fists.

"You're not Wolf," he snarled. "You are Raven, and Raven is *dead*." She started to answer, but he shouted over her. "There is no Raven! Your crew *left* you, do you

182

understand? You have no crew! Raven is dead, and *so are you!*"

Brann looked up at him, and her expression changed into a look of horror.

"Coll—" started Rieka, but Coll turned away, grabbed a tether and jumped down from Cub's side. He hit the ground hard and stumbled away.

He walked a kilometre, perhaps more, hardly knowing what he was doing. His mind was a white froth of anger – at Brann, at Rieka, at Fillan even. It was cold and he had no coat, nor any way to make a fire. It was stupid. He refused to admit it. He kept walking as night fell, and at last he slipped and settled into a hollow, half under a thorn bush. He lay there, shivering and glaring into the dark, seeing Alpha's face. She'd stared right through him. She hadn't even recognised him.

Finally, he fell asleep.

When Coll awoke, it was bright. The sun already seemed quite high in the sky, but the air was cold.

Gradually the previous day came back to him. Finding Wolf. Wolf attacking them. Alpha. Alpha staring at him, cold and blank, seeing nothing but the Construct he was in, the enemy. And then the things he'd shouted at Brann.

You have no crew.

Coll groaned and staggered to his feet. He'd been angry, of course. Brann had been taunting him, of course. And yet, in the new day, the anger was hard to hold on to. The taunting had lost its power. There were only the things he had said to her and her look of horror.

He gazed back and saw Cub on the far side of the valley. For a moment, he thought about not returning, but that was foolish. He sighed, walked back on aching, shaky legs and heaved himself aboard. Rieka and Fillan were there. Brann wasn't.

"Hey," he muttered, climbing over the deck rail.

Fillan turned. "Coll!"

He ran towards Coll, wrapped his arms round his waist and hugged him so tight Coll thought he was going to fall over.

"Hey," Coll muttered again. He felt embarrassed but oddly pleased to see the boy.

Fillan looked up. "Coll, where's Brann?"

Coll frowned. "What?" He looked up at Rieka. "What do you mean?"

Rieka hadn't moved. She stood at the far end of the deck, watching him. "Brann's gone," she said in a cold voice. "She left."

"Maybe she's just cooling off," said Coll. "Like

I, um, was."

"Her pack's gone too," said Rieka.

Coll looked at her. "Well…" he said, and stopped. He realised, with a flicker of shame, that part of him was relieved. "Well," he said again. "I mean, I guess that's her choice."

Fillan pulled back and gaped at him. "What?"

Coll shrugged. "She was never happy on Cub. She wasn't Wolf. I suppose she's … you know. Decided."

But Fillan shook his head. "No, no, we have to find her, Coll. She's one of us! She only left because you… Because…" He didn't finish. His face screwed up as if he was confused.

Coll scowled. "I'm not responsible for what she does, Fillan," he said. "She wasn't *Wolf*. She never was, do you understand? She's not our problem."

Fillan stared at him for a second, his mouth open. He took a step back.

Then he roared and charged at Coll, crashing into him.

"Hey!" spluttered Coll, almost tripping. "Ow, stop it!"

"GET HER BACK!" screamed Fillan. He bounced away from Coll, but charged again. His small arms wheeled furiously, and Coll struggled to hold him back. "GET HER *BACK*!"

"Stop this!" snapped Coll. "Fillan, don't be ridiculous!

185

Stop!" He shoved Fillan, but the boy came at him again. Coll pushed him away hard, and Fillan sprawled backwards and landed on the deck.

Coll stared down at him. "What are you doing?" he demanded.

Fillan glared up at him. Beside him, Kevin the Ant reared up on its back four legs, chittering angrily. Fillan reached for the little leather pouch round his neck, tore it loose and flung it at Coll.

Coll caught it automatically. "Fillan—"

"*Open it*," hissed Fillan.

Coll sighed and tipped the contents out into his hand.

There were the three pebbles he'd seen before, grey and water-smoothed, the ones Fillan had brought with him when he joined Wolf. Fillan, his mother, his father. But now there was also a small piece of dark brown glass, sharp and brilliant. A single black feather. And a little carved wolf's head.

Coll glanced at Rieka. Her arms were folded and she was glaring at him. He noticed her eyes were the same colour as the piece of glass. Fillan must have found this in the Glass Lands and packed it away. The black feather was from Brann's Raven cape, he realised. And the little carved head was Coll's, the one Coll had given him, long

186

ago it seemed now, in the dorm room on Wolf. He'd taken it off the chain, put it in the bag with the others. All of them together.

"She's one of us," growled Fillan. "One of *us*. *Get. Her. Back.*"

Coll studied the little items in his hand. The brown glass glinted and the feather shone almost blue. This didn't mean anything, he knew. It was just Fillan being silly. The little wooden boar's head was worn slightly, as if someone had held it tight.

"It's not that simple." He looked away around the deck, anywhere but Fillan's gaze. "I mean, it's *not*." The deck was a mix of metal and wood, plastic and anthryl. It was Cub, but it had been Raven once, hadn't it? Brann had been Raven. What was she now? Alpha had stared right through him. Was he still Wolf? What was he? What were *they*?

He stared again at the collection. After a long time, he nodded. "All right." He coughed. "All right, then. We'll get her back."

Fillan gazed up at him from the deck. "Really?"

Coll sighed. "Yes. I'm … I'm sorry. Yes."

Fillan sniffed and nodded. He stood up and brushed the dust off his cloak, the Wolf cloak he'd been so pleased with when he first came aboard. He took back the bag and stored the items carefully inside. He didn't look at Coll.

"Do you know where she went?" asked Coll.

Rieka was still glaring at him but shook her head. "There's no way of knowing."

Coll thought. "She'll have gone after Dragon," he said at last. "That's what I would do, if I were her. Dragon destroyed Raven. She thinks Dragon took the Raven crew. She was angry."

Rieka mused. "Dragon went east, after Wolf."

"Then that's where we'll go," said Coll.

"We'll have to be quick," said Rieka. "If she reaches Dragon, she doesn't have a chance."

Cub ran along the valley floor, following Dragon's huge stomping footprints as fast as they could. But the ground was uneven and potholed, and they had to pick their way between them. It was afternoon before Fillan, peering ahead, pointed and shouted, "Look!"

In front of them was a scrap of dark grey. Cub pulled to a halt and Coll and the others climbed down.

"Be careful," said Coll, holding Fillan's hand tight. The ground was riddled with holes and the sound of rushing water came from far below.

They reached the dark grey shape and Rieka picked it up. It was Brann's cloak. "Would she leave this?" she asked.

"No," said Fillan. "She—"

Coll turned. Fillan was staring at the side of one of the bigger holes. The edge of it was fresh, as if it had just opened up, and there was a track gouged into the earth. It was the mark a boot might leave, if it had slipped suddenly…

Coll leaned carefully over the hole and peered down. It seemed to go a very long way. He turned back to Rieka and Fillan. Fillan looked hopeful. Rieka's face was twisted into an unhappy, helpless expression. Coll looked at Fillan again.

"We'll need rope," he said.

19

UNDERGROUND

They tied one end of the rope to Cub, and threw the other down the hole. Rieka rooted through boxes on board Cub and came back with a clip, and she and Coll made an abseil harness. She gave him a torch on a strap round his head and checked the knots. Then Coll checked them again.

"Are you sure about this?" asked Rieka, peering down into the hole.

"No," said Coll. He shrugged and looked around. "Cub will be vulnerable with only the two of you. If anyone comes, you run, OK? Don't worry about us. We'll find our own way out."

Fillan looked worried, but Rieka nodded. "All right."

"All right," echoed Coll. He swallowed.

"Watch your arm," said Rieka.

Coll nodded. Then, before he could change his mind,

he stepped off the edge of the hole and into space.

Slowly he lowered himself into the dark. The head lamp was weak and it wobbled and shook as he descended. He peered up and saw the little white circle of light above him, and Rieka and Fillan's heads.

Down he went into the dark. Down, down. He saw an ancient tree root reaching out of the side, torn and ripped. Had Brann landed on this? Had it broken her fall? Down. The circle of light above became a dot, and now there was something below, a grey shimmer that became the ground, which was covered in gravel. There was no sign of Brann. He sank further, until at last his feet touched the ground.

He looked around. He was in a long narrow cave, and the sides were dark and rough, covered in lumpy stone. The floor was dry, but he could hear rushing water somewhere close. Perhaps from the Steel River pipe, working down through the ground?

His torch picked up a small dark mark on the stone. It was a drop of blood. He nodded, trying to control a wave of panic, and scanned the ground. He saw another drop a metre away.

So, perhaps an animal. But perhaps it was Brann – and if it *was* Brann, she was hurt but moving.

Coll unfastened his harness and tugged twice on the

rope to let them know he'd landed, and then he followed the blood. It led him slightly upwards, through a gap and into another cave. Lying on the ground was Brann.

"Brann!" Coll shouted, running towards her. She lay without moving. Her face was white. He placed a hand against her cheek and it was freezing. "Brann!"

She didn't react. He shook her and called again. And now, finally, she twitched.

Coll sagged in relief. "Brann, wake up!" he shouted.

Her face twisted into a scowl as she opened her eyes. When she saw him, she snarled.

"Go away."

She tried to roll away from him, but then yelped in pain and sat up holding her wrist. The hand was bent at a horrible unnatural angle.

"Brann, please," said Coll.

She glared at him. "I hate you."

Coll ducked his head. He didn't want to meet her gaze, but he forced himself to face her. "I'm sorry," he said. He thought of his excuses – his anger, her taunting, the situation. None of it mattered. "It was my fault, not yours. I'm so sorry."

"Why are you even *here*?" she hissed. "You *left* us."

Coll nodded again. "It was Fillan," he said. "He made me see that we're … crew. I hadn't realised, but he's right.

You're my crew. I'm your crew." He shrugged. "We're crew."

She glowered at him and then looked away. Her eyes were watering, perhaps in the glare of the torchlight.

"My wrist is broken," she said.

"We've got a rope," said Coll. "We can pull you up. Come on."

He reached under her armpits and heaved her to her feet. She was weak, and it seemed like she would fall over again, but she stayed upright. She whimpered as her hand moved.

"This way," he said, leading her back to the first cave. The sound of rushing water was suddenly much louder, and he realised it was running down the walls. The cave was filling up, and the end of the rope now lay in the middle of a pool of water half a metre deep.

Coll stepped into the water, and gasped as its icy cold clamped round his ankles like a vice. But he forced himself to wade forward and reached the end of the rope. Brann wouldn't be able to climb it with her broken wrist, so he tied the end into a loop. As he pulled it tight, he saw a small movement under the surface of the pool. A strange shape, like a rock, opening up—

"COLL!" screamed Brann, and Coll jerked back just as something snapped at him. He staggered away in astonishment and almost collided with Brann. She was staring into the water near his feet and he saw another movement. Without thinking he stepped forward and kicked as hard as he could. Something flew through the air in a spray of water and smacked against the wall with a *CLACK*! As it fell, he saw it clearly. The flattened round shape, the line of a mouth, the teeth…

A rockjaw.

Coll stared at the wall. *Lumpy*, he thought. The wall was lumpy.

Oh *no*.

"Out of the water!" he yelled. "Back, back!"

Brann stumbled away. Coll felt a sudden sharp pain in his right ankle and looked down to see one of the rockjaws had seized his shin.

"Argh!" he yelped. He reached down with his left hand and dragged it loose, leaving watery red ribbons of blood. The creature immediately turned and tried to bite his hand, its teeth skittering off the metal. Coll threw it hard against the far wall and heard it clatter.

"What do we do?" asked Brann.

Coll didn't know. All they had to do was reach the rope, but as he watched, more and more of the lumps on the wall slipped loose and fell into the pool. And more water was cascading down. Perhaps it would drain away, but how soon? He pointed his torch around and made out a sandy grey line on the cave wall about halfway up, and cursed.

"What?" asked Brann.

"I think that's how high the water goes."

Brann looked at him, and then at the grey line, and then at the pool of water, now frothing. "We have to get out of here," she muttered.

Coll nodded. He took one more look at the rope dangling down. It was so close, so *close*... But there was no way.

"Back the way you went," he said.

Brann turned and headed upwards into the next cave, and Coll limped after her. As he looked back, he saw a trail of blood coming from his ankle, seeping into the water. The pool was a metre deep now and rising fast.

The next cave was still dry, but as Coll shone his torch about he saw the grey line again. The water would seep in here too, or the pool would rise high enough to flow into it. They had to get out.

"Here!" shouted Brann at last, and Coll limped over. There was a crack in the wall, rough and narrow, leading to a tunnel. It was below the line but seemed to lead upwards.

"What do you think?" asked Brann.

Coll looked around desperately, but couldn't see any other openings. He licked a finger and held it near the crack for a few seconds. Was there a breeze? He thought perhaps there was a movement of air. Perhaps from outside... And besides, what other choice did they have?

"You first," he said. "Can you crawl?"

Brann looked at her wrist. Coll pulled off his cloak and made a sling. "This will hurt," he warned her. She nodded and he pulled it tight. She whimpered and bit her lip hard, but didn't protest. After he was done, she tested it carefully and nodded again. She could use her other arm now at least.

"Take the torch," he said, and fastened it round her head. Then he helped her climb into the crack. As she turned away, his world vanished into darkness. Just flickers of torchlight and the sound of splashing water.

Brann clambered away and he followed in the dark. How long would it take for this cave to start filling up? How long before the rockjaw creatures came after them? He tried not to think about it. The tunnel rose on a gentle slope for a metre or two. Then it levelled off and, to his despair, dipped downwards.

"Can you see anything?" he called. The walls seemed to bounce his voice back and forth until it was just distortion and noise. Brann shouted something back, but he couldn't make out the words. He could tell from her voice, though. Nothing. The tunnel narrowed and now Coll couldn't crawl on his hands and knees any more. He had to wriggle like a snake. What if he got stuck? What if it became too narrow to go any further? The thought was horrible. Stone pressed in on him from all sides and he felt suddenly terrified.

I'm a Worm, he thought out of nowhere. *I've become a Worm.* He wanted to laugh but he didn't dare. Somehow he felt that if he started laughing he might never stop.

Brann shouted something again.

"What?" he called. But before she could answer, something seeped past his knees, and then down to his hands like a cold stain. It was…

Water. The water had risen to the top of the tunnel and was now trickling down after them. How far back were the creatures? How long before they could swim and catch up with them? And then another thought – what if the water rose high enough to fill the tunnel?

He inched forward faster until his face was up against Brann's boots. He wanted to push her, but he knew that wouldn't help. But still, he wanted to, could hardly bear not to, and the water was rushing past him now. Surely it wouldn't be long—

And then there was a black space in front of him.

Brann's torch moved in a crazy pattern, then shone back into his eyes and he was blinded. He held one hand up and the light moved away. Something reached for him – he realised it was Brann just in time to hold back a scream. She pulled him out of the tunnel. He tumbled out of the tunnel, and by the light of the torch he realised they were in another cave.

It was small. A rocky mound had piled up against the far wall, and a faint light shone down on it from a gap of sky a few metres above their heads. Coll and Brann scrambled on to the mound and looked up. It was too high. Too far to reach. There was no escape.

Below them, water poured out of the tunnel and into the cave around them, forming a moat. And as it did, the first of the creatures tumbled in with it.

20

WORTHY

Water spilled into the cave around them and the rockjaw creatures followed. Ten, twenty, a hundred, their mouths open obscenely wide, frothing in the water, the cave echoing with their furious snapping. Coll and Brann stood on the rock near the back, trapped.

"Can you climb up?" asked Brann, pointing at the tiny gap of sky above them.

Coll studied the walls. They were rough. There might be handholds… Then he looked at Brann's wrist in her makeshift sling.

"What about you?"

"You could get help maybe," she said. But she was trembling and he shook his head.

"No. Stand with me – we'll hold them off."

The water was close now, dark and deadly, filled with writhing shapes.

Coll searched for a weapon, and found two thick sticks. He handed one to Brann. "Shout!" he said. "They might hear us!" Leaning back, he bellowed up to the daylight. "HELLLLLLLPPP! HELLLLLLLP!"

"HELP US!" shouted Brann. "FILLAN! RIEKA! HELP!"

A rockjaw toppled out next to Coll, and he whacked it away with his stick. Behind them, the ground banked up against the wall. Were they high enough to stay dry? He couldn't tell. The water showed no signs of slowing.

"I'm sorry," he said suddenly.

Brann turned. "What?"

"I'm sorry I said that stuff. About Raven. About … about you."

Brann gave a frightened laugh, then her face grew serious. "You came to get me."

Coll shrugged. They moved back, almost at the wall. The water around them frothed.

A creature leapt and Coll pulled back as its jaws slammed shut just millimetres from his face. It landed on the ground, opening and closing, and he kicked it away, but another one came after it, and another. They were running out of space. He felt the cave wall against his back. More creatures came for them, and Coll and Brann swept them aside, back into the water again and again.

"Argh!" screamed Brann, as one bit at her leg. Coll reached down and flung it away, but another one came, and as Coll smashed his stick down against its open mouth it *crunched* shut. The stick splintered into pieces.

And still there were more, and Coll didn't dare use his hands to fight them off. Brann was tiring; he took her stick and swung it again and again, smashing and sweeping. The little half-circle in front of them became their world, covered in blood and bits of shell, and behind it were ever more creatures, piled above each other, rolling in. His hands were slick with sweat. He drove Brann's stick down hard into the nearest one, spearing it.

The stick snapped.

Desperately Coll threw the broken stick and its speared creature among the rest. They immediately erupted into a rage of killing, turning on the injured one in a froth of red. For a brief moment, the tide of monsters receded as they fought each other. Coll panted for breath and searched for another stick.

"*Go!*" gasped Brann. "Coll, *go!*"

"I won't leave you!" he snapped.

She looked bewildered. "Why *not?*"

Coll stared at her. Part of him wondered the same thing. Brann wasn't Wolf; he owed her nothing. He wanted to run. He wanted to save himself, to clamber out of the cave. He could still do it.

But he didn't.

Alpha had stared right through him, as Wolf had attacked Cub. Stared right through him and not seen him. Like always, really. He remembered standing on Wolf's deck as they fought Raven, *heaving* at the net with the others. She'd seen him then, hadn't she? It had seemed so important that she saw him. Saw him and knew he was worthy.

He'd spent his life trying to justify himself – to Alpha, to the crew, trying to prove he was as good as everyone else. The arm, the leg. The way everyone knew he was different. He'd had to be special, when everyone else could just *be*. He had to convince the world he was good enough.

A rockjaw flipped out of the water at them; he caught it mid-flight in his left hand and threw it away, *clack*, against the cave wall. His metal arm glinted in the thin light from above. Why should he have ever thought he *wasn't* good enough? He'd done wrong, but he'd done right too. He was scared, but he was *here*.

"I won't leave you," he said again.

The rockjaws were swarming back towards the tiny spot of ground, chittering and snapping, a horrible tide of death. There was no escape. There was no weapon.

But Coll stayed.

It didn't matter if Alpha saw him. It didn't matter what Wolf's crew thought. He'd been worthy. He was still worthy.

He was worthy.

Suddenly he knew what to do. Rolling up his leggings, he unfastened his prosthetic leg and kneeled, holding it in both hands, feeling the weight of plastic and metal and anthryl, and everything it represented. Then he lifted it and swung it in a huge smash that crashed through five or more of the creatures and sent them hurtling back into the water.

"CUB!" he roared.

The leg chipped and splintered but didn't break. He held it firm and knocked the creatures away, sweeping and sweeping, screaming with defiance. "CUB! CUUBB!!"

"Coll!" shouted Brann, but he hardly heard her. All his life he'd been treated differently. All his life he'd had to prove himself. But right here, right now, there was just him and death. This was his body. Here was his crew. He swung again and again.

"Coll!"

Coll glanced up and saw to his astonishment that Brann was holding the end of a rope loop. And now he could make out two heads peering down from the gap above them – Rieka and Fillan!

"Go!" he shouted. Brann dragged the loop over her shoulders and under her arms. She tugged twice and it pulled upwards, heaving her away. The leg cracked, Coll's arms ached, but he kept going. Brann reached the top, and a few seconds later the cable tumbled down for him. He hopped up on to his one foot as the creatures flung themselves towards him, then he leapt and grabbed the rope. The remains of his leg slipped from his hand and fell into the mass of shapes below, as he rose up and out of the cave.

As he reached the top, he realised he was laughing.

Hands reached for him, Rieka's and Fillan's, pulling him out. The sun seemed incredibly bright, dazzling and white. He scrunched his eyes tight shut. He stumbled out on his hands and knees, feeling the damp grass, the breeze on his face, hearing his scraping breaths and the hammer beat of his heart.

"Coll!" shouted Fillan's voice, somehow near and yet far away. "You did it!" Then: "Where's your leg?"

Coll grinned. Every part of him ached: his arms, his chest, his shoulders, the stump of his left arm, the base of his leg where the prosthetic should be. His *hair* ached. But all he could think about was the feeling of kneeling in the cave, driving the creatures away.

"I must have left it down there," he murmured. "Get it for me, will you?"

He opened his eyes and saw Fillan glancing uncertainly at the hole. He chuckled. "It's OK, Fillan, I'm kidding."

Brann was sitting on the ground as Rieka examined her wrist. Brann was watching Coll, and he nodded to her. She bit her lip, then nodded back. Then she suddenly snarled. "Ow!"

"Well then, stop *moving*," snapped Rieka, fastening a bandage round a splint.

"Be careful!"

"Do I look like a medic? Do I? Do I have a badge that says I'm responsible for mending idiots every time they get themselves hurt?" Her words were harsh, but she wasn't looking at either of them. She seemed to be blinking a lot.

"Hey," Coll said. "Thank you."

He lay back on the grass, closed his eyes and listened to the breeze.

Rieka made him a new leg, skimming a tiny handful of anthryl from Cub and programming it to bind to some scraps of plastic and metal. It wasn't as good as his old one. It didn't feel like part of him, didn't move in the right way, and when he tested his weight, it was like a sharp stick poking into his knee. He grimaced and shrugged. It was just a leg.

"So what do we do now?" asked Brann.

Coll sighed. "Wolf needs our help," he said.

Rieka frowned, and Brann looked as if she was about to say something, but Coll raised a hand.

"Dragon is still out there, and you saw how Wolf was – she can't survive much longer. We have to help her." He looked around. "I mean, you know, *I* have to help her. If I can."

"Maybe Wolf made her choice," said Rieka. For once, her voice wasn't harsh. She said, "We did our best. We found her, but she attacked us. She doesn't *want* our help."

"Constructs don't help each other," said Brann. "It's not natural."

"Yes," said Coll. Then he said, "But different crews don't work together, and here we are. Tigers don't become Beetles, until they do." He looked at Rieka. "You said it: the way we are makes no sense. It's not how we're supposed to be. You don't have to come with me. I know you want to head back north and find that signal. You can do that, take Cub, that was the deal. But I'm going to help Wolf, if I can."

He smiled. "I wanted her to see me, you know? It's what I've always done. Tried to show her I can be as good as everyone, better than everyone. So she'd know I was worthy. But in the cave…" He remembered the feeling of fighting back the rockjaws, almost laughing. He wanted to hold on to that certainty for as long as he could.

"Alpha's a good leader," he said. "She's a good person. But she's not … a good mother." He stopped. "She tries. She looked after me. She did her best to protect me." He sighed. "But really, she's just Alpha. And that's … OK. It's not her fault; it's just how she is. How she has to be. But now I have to make my own decisions. They need us, and I'm going to help."

"I'll come with you," said Brann. She shrugged. "I don't care about helping Wolf. But Dragon's my only hope of finding my Raven crew."

Fillan said, "We'll go with you, Coll. Me and Kevin." The little metal Ant chirped and nodded.

"No, Fillan," said Coll. "You stay with Rieka. She'll keep you safe."

Rieka bristled. "Oh, what, now I'm a babysitter as well?" She chewed her lip. "Fine," she said at last. "*Fine*. Great idea. Let's go find Wolf and fight the scariest Construct in the world, just the four of us." She glowered. "Assuming we can even find it, that is."

Coll heaved himself up, carefully balancing on his new leg, and looked out over the valley.

"Maybe there's a trail we can follow," he said. "Like before."

"We've no idea where to start looking," said Brann. "And wherever it is, if you want to help, you'd better get there quick, because your Wolf was hardly hanging in there."

Coll nodded.

Brann said, "There *is* a way to do it … if you really want to."

He frowned at her. "What?"

Brann said nothing, only grinned at him, and suddenly Coll realised what she meant.

"Oh no," he said in dismay. "No, absolutely not. *No!*"

21

CUB

"Flap the wings harder!" shouted Brann. "Not like that – get a rhythm!"

Coll had no idea what she meant. His eyes were tight shut and his hands gripped his harness. Part of him could see through Cub's eyes, but he didn't want to, because that meant looking at the ground, and the ground was, oh, the ground was *so far away*—

"Concentrate!" snapped Brann. "All together, down and up, down and up!"

Coll swallowed, and tried to join in with the others as they flapped Cub's … *wings*? Because Cub wasn't a wolf cub any more. His body was thinner, his back legs bony, his short stubby tail now a wide fan, his head long and his mouth a beak. And his front legs were *wings* now, spreading wide to catch the air currents, the claws gone, the toes stretched and flattened…

"Down-and-up," Coll muttered breathlessly. "Down-and-up, down-and-up, down-and-up—" As he said the words, Cub's new wings flapped awkwardly and the Construct limped through the sky in a staggering trail.

"That's it!" shouted Brann encouragingly. "We're doing it! Down and up, that's it, nice and smooth!" She laughed. "See, flying is easy! Just remember that if you ever stop, you'll die." Coll opened his eyes and stared at her, and she grinned. "I'm joking! That's a Raven joke. It's funny, see?"

"Funny," Rieka gasped. "But also true, right?"

Brann flapped a hand and shrugged. "Oh, *kind* of. But really, you've got ages when you're falling. Five seconds, maybe even more. Down-and-up, everyone! Down-and-up! We'll reach some air currents soon!"

Cub lurched though the air over the valley. It was weirdly quiet: no sound of wind, just the creak of joints as the Construct's wings beat. Tentatively Coll peered down. They'd travelled a kilometre already, and the whole valley was spread before him, and beyond were small hills and forests and rivers and the remains of old settlements…

"See?" murmured Brann. "Like Raven." Her whole face was different here in the air. Her hair was swept back, her skin glowed and her eyes gleamed with focus as if she was mapping out the sky around them. She smiled, and despite his terror Coll smiled back.

"What's that?" asked Rieka.

Cub turned his bird head and peered down and Coll saw through his eyes to a trail carved through a small wood. Broken trees stared up like scars in the landscape, and on the far side of the wood—

"It's them!" shouted Fillan. "Coll, it's them!"

Dragon and Wolf were fighting.

Wolf seemed even more gaunt from here, straggly and desperate, losing ground with every step. Dragon was huge and covered in armour plating. It looked indestructible. It looked like nothing could stop it, ever. It struck again and again, driving Wolf back towards a cliff edge.

"Go!" shouted Coll. "Come on, go!"

Cub tumbled downwards and Brann swore as the crew lost their rhythm. Coll could feel her trying to keep control of Cub's shape. "We need power!" she roared.

Coll understood. He tried to pour his faith into their little Construct. "Cub!" he roared. "Cub!"

"Cub!" shouted Fillan, and Rieka too. Cub's wings pulled into a dive and he steadied, studying his prey, aiming for Dragon's head. "CUB!" shouted the crew.

Dragon didn't notice until almost too late. It reared its head back in surprise and Cub's beak narrowly missed its eyes, instead gouging a scar across its snout. Cub tried to claw at Dragon's face, but Dragon swung its huge muzzle and smashed against the smaller Construct, sending them hurtling through the air and crashing to the ground.

Coll and the others were thrown from side to side. The gyroscopes and stabilisers screamed, trying to absorb the impact, but Coll's ears rang and his shoulders ached from the harness straps.

He stared up at Dragon as it lumbered towards them. "Move," he muttered, but Brann just shook her head in confusion. She seemed stunned.

Coll stared at her. "Wolf shape!" he roared suddenly. "We need to be wolf shape again!" He pushed his thoughts down into the Construct. Dragon raised a mighty foot to crush them—

Cub transformed back into wolf form, his wings becoming legs again, his feathers turning into fur. Coll felt Fillan's willpower join his, and their Construct scrambled away on four legs just as the foot smashed down.

Dragon stopped and leaned back. It gazed at them, tipping its head as if surprised. But then it rumbled forward again, and the ground trembled under its massive weight.

They couldn't fight like this, Coll thought. On the ground Dragon would destroy them…

"We need to fly again!" he shouted. "Brann, think Raven! Give us wings!"

Brann nodded and closed her eyes. Cub's front feet splayed back out into wings and flapped, and Coll desperately counted *down-and-up, down-and-up* as the little Construct fluttered into the air. Dragon stopped again, watching them.

"Lead it round!" Coll ordered, and Brann guided Cub through the air behind Dragon, forcing it to turn. They tried to swoop, but Dragon reared up more quickly than they expected, and they pulled back again. Dragon's stubby wings flapped as if trying to lift it into the air, but it was too armoured now, too heavy to fly.

"We're safe here!" Brann shouted.

But Dragon's tail suddenly whipped round like a mace. They only just pulled back in time; Coll watched the spiked tail swish past a metre away, and the force of the air sent them tumbling.

Then Dragon gave a surprised snarl, almost a yelp. It turned back and Coll saw – Wolf was attacking!

She had leapt while Dragon was distracted, and now her huge jaws crunched down on Dragon's head. She seemed to have had a surge of energy, and was clawing and scraping in fury. Brann steadied Cub, lifted them up high, and brought the little Construct down like an arrow,

213

faster and faster. They slammed into Dragon's back, Cub's long sharp beak gouged into the armour, and Coll shuddered as he felt the collision through every bone in his body.

Dragon's hide buckled, twisted – and ripped open!

The Construct roared in fury, perhaps even in pain, and it shook itself violently. Cub tumbled to the ground again, sorting his wings just enough to slow his fall before he landed.

"Wolf shape again!" shouted Coll. "Lose the wings!"

Cub's wings became paws, racing forward along the ground out of Dragon's reach. And now, behind them, the real Wolf was attacking again! She seized Dragon's back, aiming for the torn armour, trying to worry it loose.

Coll, battered and dizzy, checked the others. "Is everyone all right?" he bellowed.

Brann swore very loudly. Fillan stuck up a thumb. Kevin was tucked under his arm and making excited *chick-chick*s. But Rieka shook her head.

"It's not enough," she muttered. "Dragon's just too big, Coll. It's not *enough*."

Coll stared up at the massive Construct. Even as he watched, it hurled Wolf away and she slammed into the trees with a yelp. Rieka was right. Between them, all they'd managed was to buckle one piece of armour, and

they'd been lucky. If Dragon got one solid hit on them…
It was so big and heavy, indomitable, almost tottering on
its dragon legs under the huge weight of armour. Coll felt
a sympathetic pain in his knee as his new prosthetic dug
into him. He was still unsteady with it…

He looked down. "Fillan? Can you be … Boar?"

The others stared at him. "Boar?" asked Fillan. He
frowned for a moment, then nodded. "I can be Boar.
Boar… *Yes*."

Dragon heaved forward. Coll said, "*Now*, Fillan. Do it
now and aim for its ankles. Do it *now*!"

Cub ran towards Dragon. As he did so, Fillan closed his
eyes and the little Construct changed mid-run. His head
spread wider and thicker, becoming ridged and powerful.
Long, thick tusks with razor-sharp tips grew up and out
of his mouth, and his body became barrel-shaped, his
legs short but powerful—

"BOAR!" shouted Fillan.

Dragon swung its head down but Cub slipped
underneath, dipped his head and *smashed* hard into
Dragon's front-right leg, with the speed of a wolf and
the force of a boar. There was the horrible sound of
splintering metal, and Dragon yelped and stumbled back
in surprise and pain.

"BOOOAR!" screamed Fillan in triumph.

Dragon scrambled backwards, trying to reach underneath itself to get to this aggravating tiny Construct, but Cub was too fast. He sped up again and smashed into the same leg, actually leaping off the ground and jabbing with his tusks. "BOOAR!"

Dragon stumbled back again. It bellowed with rage, swiping down, retreating. It raised a front paw and swatted Cub with a lucky blow and Coll's world flipped.

"Argh!" Cub tumbled over and over and crashed to the ground. Coll gasped, but Fillan screamed defiance and Cub jumped to his feet and thundered back in. Dragon prepared to attack, but then snarled – Wolf was attacking from the other side!

As Dragon turned to deal with Wolf, Cub smashed at its legs again. Dragon was forced back.

"BOOOARR!" screamed Fillan. His face was red, spittle ran down his chin, and his eyes gleamed with mad joy. "BOOOAR! RAM! SMASH! CRASH! BOAAAAAAAAAAAR!"

Dragon moved back again. It hit Cub once more, but Cub shook it off and dashed right back in. But in that moment Dragon had time to regain its balance and it moved its feet—

—and only then did it seem to realise it was on the edge of the cliff.

One back claw scraped desperately at the air where the ground ended. The other dug in as it tried to recover its balance, but Wolf lunged from one side and Dragon had to rear up to defend itself. Cub charged once more and smashed at its legs, again, again, until it stepped back…

The cliff edge gave way, and Dragon fell.

It scrabbled desperately with its front paws, before disappearing. Cub rushed forward and they saw the Construct tumble, crashing against the cliff, scraping and flailing, spinning in mid-air as it tried to control its wings, but it was too late and not enough…

It hit the ground fifty metres below with a *BOOM* that Coll felt through his feet. Metal and plastic armour plates exploded into the air and scattered with the force of the crash, and there was a sickening *crack*, like bones breaking all together, and Dragon lay still.

Cub and Wolf stared down. Fillan was panting and his hands were clenched in tight fists, his skin mottled and red and his hair wild. Coll rested one hand on his shoulder and the boy jumped, snarled, glared at Coll and then blinked in confusion.

"Is it … dead?" whispered Brann.

Coll bit his lip. "I think—"

Dragon moved.

It clambered back to its feet. One long ear was torn off,

one leg was twisted, and the armour plating on its back was ripped and torn. The Construct lifted its head and stared up at them, and its stubby thick wings fluttered once or twice. Then it took a limping step, and another, and another. And slowly, painfully, it dragged itself away.

22

CREWS

Wolf and Cub stared at each other at the edge of the cliff.

Wolf had taken more damage. The armour plating on her left flank was ripped half off and was flapping like a scab. Beneath it, pistons and mechanics dripped with oil, and ribbons of anthryl hung loose. But still, she seemed stronger than earlier. The victory over Dragon would have restored her crew's faith, and she was riding on that energy. Her sides heaved and her lips were pulled back into a snarl. She seemed to be deciding whether to attack.

"Brann, take us up," said Coll.

Cub changed shape around them, his wings stretching and flapping, and the little Construct rose until it reached Wolf's eyeline. Wolf pulled back.

Coll unstrapped his harness and limped forward, rubbing his knee. He stood tall on Cub's shoulders and waved. At first, nothing happened. Then an armoured panel moved aside near Wolf's head, and a woman stepped out. She stood and stared at Coll for several seconds.

Then she waved back.

They met halfway between the two Constructs. Alpha, Dolph and Rudy on one side, Cub's crew on the other. Kevin the Ant sat draped round Fillan's shoulder, chittering to itself. Alpha's arm seemed to be the only thing wrong with her, but Rudy's head was covered in tight wound bandages, and Dolph had brought him a seat. He sank into it and smiled at Coll.

For a few seconds, no one said anything. Alpha studied Coll, her face carefully blank.

Coll wasn't sure how he felt. He'd spent so long getting back to Wolf, and here they were. And here was Alpha… And yet it wasn't what he'd imagined. How had he thought she would react?

He remembered the way she'd stared at him from the crack in Wolf's armour – stared right at him and somehow not recognised him. Because she was Wolf and Coll had been Cub. That was all she'd seen, he realised. She was Wolf's Alpha. Anything that wasn't Wolf was nothing. Even…

Even Coll.

He thought about what he'd said to Rieka. A good Alpha. A good person even. She'd provided for him, protected him from a crew who didn't want him aboard. Used resources – valuable anthryl – to keep him alive. She had cared for him. Did she love him? She loved her crew, and he was part of her crew. Some people could manage more, but some couldn't. She'd done the best she could.

It was enough.

"Hi," he said.

"What happened to your leg?" she asked. Her voice was guarded.

Coll shrugged. "I lost it. Still getting used to this one. It's fine." It was agony actually, but he tried not to show it. He wished he'd thought to bring a chair himself. Alpha nodded, and then examined Cub's crew one by one. Rieka, Brann, Fillan, even Kevin – she gave nothing away as she studied them.

"And you've … joined this Construct?" she asked. "What is it anyway? Why does it keep *changing*?" Her lips pursed, as if she found the idea slightly disgusting.

"It's Cub," said Coll. "It used to be Raven. We fixed it to come and find you."

Alpha frowned. "Why?"

Coll opened and closed his mouth. *Why?*

221

Behind Alpha, Rudy shook his head and sighed, and gave Coll a rueful smile.

"Because … I wanted to get back to Wolf," said Coll. "And you needed help. We came to save you."

"Coll's our Alpha," said Fillan.

Coll blinked in surprise and Alpha raised an eyebrow.

"Well, you're here," she said. "So. Good timing – we could use the anthryl."

For a moment, Coll didn't understand what she meant. At his side Brann bristled. Coll said, "We're not giving you Cub."

Alpha gave a chuckle without any humour. "This is a strange situation," she said in a firm voice. "But let me be clear. I am Wolf. *You* are Wolf. We do what we need for Wolf. If that means dismantling that … *thing* for parts, then I won't even hesitate. Understand?"

Coll frowned. Alpha was right, of course. But… He glanced at the little leather bag round Fillan's neck.

"Cub is … not Wolf," he said. He nodded. "And this is my crew."

"If you're not with us, you're our enemy," Alpha snapped. "It's that simple. It doesn't *matter* who you are – if you're not Wolf, you are *nothing*."

Coll shrugged. "Maybe. Or maybe we're stronger as a pack…"

Alpha frowned. Behind her, Dolph looked confused, but Rudy was smiling to himself.

Alpha said, "You honestly don't think we're going to work *together*, do you? You give us that thing or we will *take* it!"

"*You?*" retorted Brann. "You *threaten* us after we just saved you? That mangy old mutt can barely even stand up! Just try it and we'll—"

"It's OK," said Coll softly.

Brann glared at him, but stopped.

Coll turned back. "Repair Wolf," he said to Alpha. "There are plenty of Dragon remains down there to scavenge. We won't attack, but you won't either. We're done here."

Alpha glared at him.

"Reckon the boy's right," said Rudy in a mild tone.

Alpha turned. Coll couldn't see the expression on her face, though he could guess. But Rudy just gazed back at her calmly, and eventually she turned back. Her mouth moved as if she was chewing something unpleasant.

"You have until we're repaired," she said. "If we see you again, we won't hesitate. You are *not* Wolf." She turned and strode away.

Rudy heaved himself to his feet and winked at Coll. "Good luck, lad," he said.

"Thanks, Rudy," said Coll. "Look after her for me."

He wasn't sure if he meant Wolf or Alpha.

They watched the others return to Wolf and climb aboard.

"Are you OK?" asked Rieka.

Coll nodded. "Yeah. I mean … I will be."

"She's a good Alpha," said Rieka. "She tries to be a good person. She's just…"

He nodded. "I know."

Brann said, "Don't you want to join your crew again?"

Coll thought. Luna was there, of course. And Rudy. And he'd missed some of the others. He'd thought they were his life. He'd thought he lived for Wolf. Now he gazed at Cub sitting in the pale sunshine, and at Brann and the others.

"Maybe it's like Namir said," he said. "Maybe in the end you have to find your own crew."

They walked on. Coll's leg was still hurting, though he was getting the hang of it and the anthryl was starting to respond. It would take a while to get used to the new.

"What do we do now?" asked Fillan.

Brann said, "Dragon was my only chance to find the Raven crew."

Rieka said, "Dragon came from the north and headed

back north. The signal came from the north. I think they're connected." She frowned. "Brann, you said there was something wrong with Dragon, and you're right. The way it attacks, how powerful it is… Its deck was sealed the whole time; we never even saw the crew once. It's not like the other Constructs."

"Neither are we," said Coll.

"You could still join Wolf," said Rieka. "You and Fillan. We'll take Cub and strip him down for two people."

They reached the Construct, and Coll grabbed a cable. "If you go, we go," he said. "Right, Fillan?"

"We're Cub," said Fillan.

They strapped themselves in. Coll turned to Brann and grinned. "Ready?"

She grinned back. "Ready."

Cub stood and stretched, then shook his head and rolled his shoulders. Brann closed her eyes, and Cub stretched again, and again…

Then he lifted his wings, hopped forward and flew. Up and up, over Wolf and her crew staring at them, over the wreckage from Dragon's fall, up, until the air was clear and pure and free, and then he picked an air current and turned…

To the north.

AUTHOR'S NOTE

I Am Wolf is an idea that's been bouncing around my head for ages, in a few different forms. I loved the thought of these huge mechanical beasts roaming the land, carrying their crews on their backs, fighting and roaring and all driven to believe in the same thing – Wolf, Wolf, *Wolf!* But I didn't have a character to push it forward, until Coll came along.

Sometimes, if you're really lucky, characters just arrive in your head ready to go. It's like a knock at the door and when you open it, there they are, tapping their watch, saying, "Hurry up and put me in your book already!" Coll was like that. From the moment he appeared, I knew all about him. Coll is strong, tall, a bit hot-headed, sometimes grumpy, maybe not the smartest, but very loyal and brave, with a prosthetic arm and leg. And that was him – and I just *knew* that he was the star of the story.

But I also knew that I had to do him justice.

Representation really matters. Everyone should be able to see themselves as the hero of their stories. Coll is the hero of this story and his limb difference is one part of him, but not the *point* of him. I hope I told it right. But I don't have a limb difference, or personal experience to draw on. I knew I would need help to make Coll feel real to people who actually understood what it was like.

Fortunately, my publishers Nosy Crow were brilliant. They understood how important it was to be authentic and reached out to some amazing organisations who support kids with limb differences, like LimbBo Foundation https://limbbofoundation.co.uk/ and Finding Your Feet https://findingyourfeet.net/. I shared Coll's story with them, and they took time and care to help me understand the things I'd missed or got wrong. Thank you, all of you – you made Coll real.

In particular, huge thanks to Jane Hewitt, who invited us to the LimbBo Adventure Day where I got to meet and chat with kids and hear about their experiences. Coll's prosthetics are more advanced than the ones currently available, but there is incredible progress being made all the time. And watching wearers adapt even simple mechanisms to perform complicated manoeuvres was extraordinary. Thank you everyone for your patience and humour as I pestered you with endless tech questions – you made my geeky heart very happy!

And while I'm thanking people... Thank you so much Zöe Griffiths, my editor, for your enthusiasm, guidance and determination to do right by Coll. The cover was designed by Ray Tierney and illustrated by Karítas Gunnarsdóttir, and it is UNBELIEVABLY COOL – thank you!

But there are so many more people involved in turning my scribbles into something sensible! So if you've ever wondered who does what, *Wolf* also involved...

Kirsty Stansfield, Fiction Publishing Director

Halimah Manan, Assistant Editor

Jennie Roman, Copyeditor

Jessica White, Proofreader

Sîan Taylor, Publicist

Ian Lamb, Marketer

Xeni Soteriou, Digital Marketer

Lara Kelly, Digital Marketer

Stephanie McClelland, Production Controller

(and many more – thank you!)

Thanks also to all the people around me for help and encouragement – the good folks of Visible Ink, Adam and everyone at Argonaut Books (which you should check out if you find yourself in Edinburgh), my agent Caroline

Montgomery, who somehow stays calm whenever I'm flapping around, and to the Scottish Book Trust – your support has allowed me to visit schools and libraries across the country and chat to kids I'd never get to meet otherwise. And Catherine – always, and for everything.

Alastair
Edinburgh, 2023

LOOK OUT FOR
MORE BOOKS BY
ALASTAIR CHISHOLM

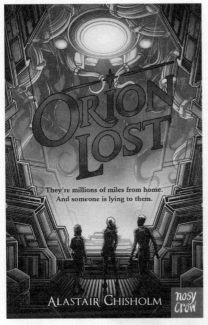

ORION LOST

They're millions of miles from home.
And someone is lying to them.

ALASTAIR CHISHOLM

nosy crow

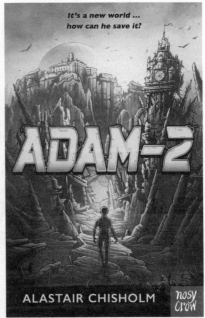

It's a new world …
how can he save it?

ADAM-2

ALASTAIR CHISHOLM

nosy crow

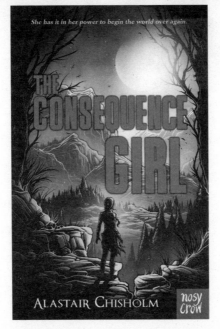

She has it in her power to begin the world over again.

THE CONSEQUENCE GIRL

ALASTAIR CHISHOLM

nosy crow

FIND OUT WHAT HAPPENS
TO COLL IN...

I AM
RAVEN

COMING SOON!